"You did a pretty good job of ending our relationship all by yourself."

He'd wondered when they would get around to talking about that. "Things weren't always what they seemed that summer."

Her gaze was very direct. "It seemed pretty clear to me."

"Two sides to every story," he said. "But maybe now isn't the best time to get into all that." He frowned. "Stay in the city for a few days."

She frowned right back at him. "Why don't you want me here? What is it you're not telling me?"

"It's not a matter of what I want," he said. "You'll be safer in Atlanta."

"Safe from what?"

"Safe from your mother's killer," he said bluntly. "Don't you get it? Your inheritance not only makes you a suspect. It may also make you a target."

THE SECRET OF SHUTTER LAKE

AMANDA STEVENS

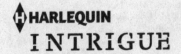

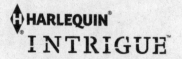

ISBN-13: 978-1-335-59062-6

The Secret of Shutter Lake

Harlequin Enterprises ULC
22 Adelaide St. West, 41st Floor
Toronto, Ontario M5H 4E3, Canada
www.Harlequin.com

Printed in U.S.A.

Recycling programs for this product may not exist in your area.

Amanda Stevens is an award-winning author of over fifty novels, including the modern gothic series The Graveyard Queen. Her books have been described as eerie and atmospheric and "a new take on the classic ghost story." Born and raised in the rural South, she now resides in Houston, Texas, where she enjoys binge-watching, bike riding and the occasional margarita.

Books by Amanda Stevens

Harlequin Intrigue

Pine Lake
Whispering Springs
Digging Deeper
The Secret of Shutter Lake

A Procedural Crime Story

Little Girl Gone
John Doe Cold Case
Looks That Kill

An Echo Lake Novel

Without a Trace
A Desperate Search
Someone Is Watching

Twilight's Children

Criminal Behavior
Incriminating Evidence
Killer Investigation

Visit the Author Profile page at Harlequin.com.

CAST OF CHARACTERS

Abby Dallas—When a discovery at the bottom of Shutter Lake turns her world upside down, she hires the man who abandoned her ten years ago to help find her mother's killer.

Wade Easton—For ten years, he's kept his father's secret in order to protect his mother. Now he has to wonder if in keeping that secret, he's unwittingly shielded a killer.

Sam Easton—Was he the mysterious man in Eva Dallas McRae's life?

James McRae—The betrayed husband who still lives in Eva's house and runs her business.

Lydia McRae—The bitter stepdaughter despised Eva for breaking up her family.

Brie Fortier—Abby's best friend has always cleaned up after her trouble-making twin brother. How far is she willing to go to protect him?

Brett Fortier—His insurance claim brings Wade Easton to the lake to investigate a missing boat. His dangerous past puts Abby in the line of fire.

Chapter One

Patches of sunlight filtered down through the murky water as Wade Easton skimmed along the lakebed. His scuba flippers kicked up a cloud of sediment and spooked a flathead catfish feeding on bottom sludge. Wade hung suspended until the residue settled, taking a moment, as he always did, to enjoy the underwater solitude. Overhead, a sunfish swam by, the blue-green coloration striking when the beam from his head lamp hit its scales. For a moment, he swam a few feet below the elongated body in complete synchronization until the fish darted away and became lost in the underwater twilight.

The bottom of the lake was littered with boulders and man-made debris, mostly cans and bottles, but every now and then, he'd spy something a little more interesting, like a lost watch or cell phone. Despite his innate curiosity, he left the items where he found them. He wasn't treasure-hunting today—not that kind of treasure—and he wasn't equipped to pick up litter. That task would fall to another diver on another day. With any luck, his meticulous research would lead him to a sunken high-end speed boat conservatively valued at a quarter of a million dollars. The kind of luxury vessel one frequently admired at a Miami Beach boat show but rarely spotted on a lake in southern Alabama.

The thirty-eight-foot stunner had been reported stolen two weeks ago, just days after the vessel had been brought up from the Gulf and berthed at a local marina. Wade had his suspicions about that theft. His gut told him the boat may have been scuttled with something even more valuable onboard. Possibly cash, possibly drugs, possibly both. He hoped to soon find out.

He moved languorously through the water, keeping an eye on his gauges, though descending to forty feet in a freshwater lake was far less risky than the deep-sea dives he'd once relished. If anything went wrong, he could ditch his equipment and swim to the surface without fear of decompression sickness or nitrogen narcosis. He could literally follow the sunbeams.

However, in his line of work, he'd learned the hard way the danger of being lulled into a false sense of security. He was diving alone, so precautions had to be taken. No one even knew he was back in town, much less at the bottom of Shutter Lake.

A shadow passing overheard startled him. He

glanced up, wondering if his empty boat had been spotted, but it was too early for most recreationists to be out on the water. The mist that had hovered over the glassy surface at daybreak was just starting to burn off when he'd set out. The forty-five-minute boat ride had taken him to the far north end of the lake, miles from the condos and marinas that populated the more picturesque southern end. Since the old bridge had been condemned and later demolished, no one came back this way except for the occasional sport fisherman trolling for a lucky spot. If someone wanted to sink an expensive speed boat, nestling it among the abandoned pylons and iron girders would be a good place to hide it.

He checked his air pressure. Still in good shape, and he had another tank in the boat if he needed more time. Might turn out to be a wasted morning, but for now, he'd keep looking. Wouldn't be the first time a hunch had sent him on a wild-goose chase, but his instincts were more reliable these days. As an independent investigator hired by the kind of insurance companies that covered expensive toys like private jets, sports cars and custom-made speed boats, he'd developed an almost sixth sense for sniffing out fraud.

Not that he needed to do much sniffing in this case. For all the pristine scenery, Shutter Lake had always had a seamy underbelly of corruption. The countless small businesses that catered to an influx of tourists every summer—marinas, bait stores, boat and equipment rentals, repair shops, restaurants, hotels, bed-and-breakfasts, camp-grounds, food trucks, dinner cruises, souvenir vendors and so on—provided endless vehicles for laundering the drug money that traveled inland from the Gulf Coast. Those opportunities coupled with the scruples of the man who claimed his boat had been stolen, and Wade definitely had his doubts.

For as long as he'd known Brett Fortier, the man had been an operator, using his charm, looks and family connections to skirt the law. Sinking an expensive boat for the insurance money and then claiming the vessel had been stolen was right in his wheelhouse. All he had to do was live off the insurance money until things quieted down and then dive down and collect the booty he'd hidden onboard.

Another shadow passed overhead. This time Wade didn't bother checking the surface but kept gliding through the water, searching for the spot he'd scoped out using aerial photography and sonar. Might be nothing more than abandoned wreckage from the smashed bridge, but he wouldn't know until—

Hold on.

Something large rested on the bottom of the lake. Adrenaline bubbles gushed upward as he maneuvered around a mound of twisted metal and concrete.

Not a boat, after all, but a luxury coupe. The discovery sent a thrill of alarm up Wade's spine. He recognized the vehicle—or thought he did. Despite the old money in the area and the more recent invasion of new wealth, a Rolls Royce Wraith wasn't a common sight in Fairhope, Alabama, much less at the bottom of Shutter Lake.

Memories assailed him as he approached the vehicle from the rear. Ten years ago, a wealthy woman named Eva Dallas McRae had vanished after putting her affairs in order, packing her bags and leaving a note for her only child, instructing the seventeen-year-old not to come looking for her. She'd fallen deeply in love and wanted a fresh start somewhere far away from Shutter Lake, far away from the obligations and expectations of her family. She'd left behind a devastated daughter, a betrayed husband and an endless wave of gossip and resentment that still simmered in certain quarters of the town to this day.

Wade took a moment to control his breathing. After the initial shock, he was keen to explore. He checked for a license plate, but the metal tag had probably rusted through and fallen off the vehicle years ago. After a cursory search of the lakebed, he moved back up to peer through the rear window. He couldn't see much. A decade of pressure and slime had taken a toll.

Another sunfish swam by, iridescent in the glow of his dive light as he circled the car. He became all too aware of the silence. Like a tomb. No sound at all except for a dull roar in his ears. He told himself he could be mistaken about the owner. No way to know for certain without checking the registration, a difficult task since both front and rear tags were missing and any VIN etchings would be concealed by layers of rust and grunge. Somehow the car had miraculously escaped damage from falling bridge debris only to be slowly eaten away by time and corrosion.

Still, there was no mistaking the flying lady hood ornament—the Spirit of Ecstasy—that remained intact. He swam up to the driver's side, wondering if he could get the door open. Maybe there was some form of identification inside. He grasped the handle as he pressed his face against the glass, trying to get a look at the secrets that might still be hidden inside.

What the...?

He jerked back in shock as another burst of bubbles shot to the surface.

The skeletal remains floated eerily behind the steering wheel, the empty eye sockets staring straight ahead as if focusing on a destination that only the dead could see.

Wade steadied his pulse and moved back in, angling the beam through the glass. He thought at first the seat belt must have kept the skeleton in place. Without restraint, the body would have floated upward. Then his light caught the flash of steel around the left wrist bone.

Sometime before the car went over the bridge, the driver had been handcuffed to the steering wheel.

ABIGAIL DALLAS STEPPED through the French doors and carefully placed the breakfast tray of coffee, fruit and assorted pastries on the glass-topped table before joining her friend, Brie Fortier, at the wrought iron railing that encased the flagstone terrace.

Another day in paradise.

No heels, no suits, no ringing cell phone or long-winded meetings to sit through. What a luxury to step from the shower and don the day's attire of shorts, sandals and T-shirt. Not that the reprieve would last forever. She hadn't returned to her hometown to lounge around the lake for the next few weeks. She was here to pitch in until her stepfather was back on his feet. A lot of hard and unpleasant work lay ahead of her. Not today, though. Not tomorrow, either, but come Monday morning, she planned to hit the ground running.

Breathing in the lake air, she trailed her gaze down the stone steps to the private dock, where a small vessel bobbed against the bumpers. Later, she'd take the boat out for a leisurely ride. The shady cove was still quiet, but the lake beyond was already ablaze with tempting sunlight. By midafternoon, the temperature and humidity would climb so high that anywhere except in the water or under the AC would become extremely uncomfortable, but for now, an early morning breeze cooled the terrace and perfumed the air with oleander. She listened to the gentle rustle of the palm fronds and banana trees and wondered again why she'd stayed away for so long. She was a Dallas, after all. Her ancestors had helped found Fairhope, or so she'd always been told. Her roots ran as deep as Shutter Lake. Yet the night she left town, she'd sworn never to return.

Never say never.

"You hear that?" Brie leaned out over the railing and cocked her head toward the water. A strand of pale blond hair came loose from the bun at her nape and coiled at her temple. Abby marveled at how little her friend had changed in ten years. Still as slender and tanned and gorgeous as the day they'd graduated high school. Still with a furrow of anxiety across her brow, no matter her professional success or personal happiness.

"Sirens," she pronounced grimly as she shot Abby an uneasy glance. "I heard one earlier, too. Sounds like the whole damn police department has been called out."

Abby lifted a hand to shade her eyes as she

peered across the water toward Lakeside Drive. "I wonder what happened."

"Some kind of accident, most likely. It's the weekend, so a lot of people are out on the water. You know how that goes. Booze, boats. Boats, booze. Seems like every summer we have at least one major catastrophe."

Abby shivered. "I should be accustomed to the wail of sirens after living in Atlanta for ten years, but somehow the sound seems more ominous down here."

"That's because when you hear a siren in a small town, you know there's a good chance that tragedy has befallen a friend or an acquaintance. Or, God forbid, a loved one." The wrinkle in her brow deepened as if something had just occurred to her.

"What's wrong?" Abby asked.

"Nothing. It's just… I can't help wondering where my brother is right now. I tried calling him earlier. He didn't pick up. Which isn't unusual for Brett. He's never been a morning person. I know it's irrational to worry, but every time I hear a siren, I can't help thinking about the time the police came to our house in the middle of the night. I heard the sirens long before they showed up. I remember lying in bed, shivering from a premonition that had plagued me all day."

"Do you have a premonition now?" Abby asked.

"No…not really."

"Then stop worrying. The accident happened years ago. Brett was a reckless kid with a fast car. He's a grown man now."

"As if anything has really changed," Brie grumbled. "You'd think a near-death experience would have taught him a valuable lesson, but the only difference now is that his toys have gotten even faster and a lot more expensive. My brother is what you'd call an adrenaline junkie, whereas I—"

"You're the sensible twin," Abby said. "You always have been."

Brie winced. "Gets a little old if you want to know the truth. Just once, I'd like to be the care-free sibling."

"Then you wouldn't be you." Abby nodded to the phone clutched in Brie's hand. "Call him again if it'll make you feel better."

"That's the thing. It probably won't. If my call goes to voicemail, I'll just fret even more." She released another heavy sigh. "At some point, I have to quit mothering him. I know that. Like you said, he's a grown man, nearly thirty years old. And he was born two minutes earlier than me, so technically, I'm the little sister. He should be watching out for me."

"Just admit it," Abby teased. "You've always enjoyed bossing him around."

"For all the good it does." Brie's smile seemed strained.

Abby turned to her friend. "What's really going on? It's not just the sirens putting you on edge, is it?"

"Am I still that easy to read?" Brie glanced at her. "I don't want to dump my problems on you. You've got enough on your plate."

"You're not dumping anything on me. I want to help. Just tell me what's wrong."

Brie bit her lip, then shrugged. "It's nothing. Just a client that's been irritating me more than usual. As for Brett, he probably turned off his phone so that he could sleep in. I'm sure he's fine."

Abby didn't press. Something was obviously troubling Brie, but for whatever reason, she wasn't yet ready to confide in her. Fair enough. They'd been best friends in high school and had kept in touch off and on during Abby's ten-year absence, but they were no longer confidants. Rebuilding that kind of trust would take time. "We don't even know for certain there's been an accident," she said. "Could be a robbery or a drug bust. Lydia says there's been a lot of cartel activity around the lake lately."

Brie rolled her eyes. "As if the cartels have even heard of this place. We're a thousand miles from the border, last time I checked. And as for your stepsister, I wouldn't put too much stock in anything coming out of her mouth. Lydia McRae always has an ulterior motive for everything she says and does. Don't you forget that. She'll paint as bleak a picture as she can of this place just to try and keep you from moving back here permanently."

"I don't think she was trying to scare me off. It was just an offhand comment in an email." Abby didn't understand the need to defend her stepsister. The two had never been close, far from it. Lydia had had a chip on her shoulder for as long as Abby could remember. She'd begrudged everything about her father's marriage to Abby's mother, and she'd made no bones about her dislike of her new stepsister. She'd resented Abby's friends, her popularity and especially her inheritance. When they were first introduced, Abby had been excited by the prospect of an older sister, someone with whom she could share secrets and their wardrobes. She'd quickly learned it was easier to avoid Lydia altogether than to try and befriend her. Brie was probably right about motive, but Abby didn't want her to be.

"You've always underestimated her," Brie said. "I've never understood why. Especially after all the hateful things she said to you when your mother left. I've had a few business dealings with her over the years, and I can tell you without a shadow of a doubt, she's still as bitter and unpleasant as she ever was."

"She's been cordial to me so far," Abby said.

"Which makes her even more dangerous. I'll say it again. Don't let down your guard around Lydia McRae, and don't let her get under your skin. She may think she's the boss, but you're in charge. Almost all the real estate holdings belong to the Dallas side of the family, including the house James and Lydia still live in. Your mother was successful before she and James married. Any wealth accumulated prior to the wedding still belongs to her. Just because father and daughter have been running the company for the past ten years doesn't mean they've got a legitimate claim to her prewedding assets. Or to yours."

"It's tricky," Abby said. "Technically, Mother and James are still married. As far as I know, neither of them ever filed for a divorce. As for my claim…" She paused. "I left town, too. I abandoned the business just like my mother did."

"No, you didn't. You went to live with your grandmother in Atlanta. You were only seventeen. No one expected you to step in and fill your mother's shoes at that age."

"I could have come back after college."

"Coulda, woulda, shoulda." Brie gave a dismissive shrug. "You're home now and I, for one, am thrilled to have you back. You know I'm here for you, right? Anything you need, just say the word. I'm a damned good real estate attorney if I do say so myself."

"I appreciate that."

Brie turned and plucked a fresh strawberry from a crystal bowl before pouring herself a cup of coffee and stirring in creamer. "Speaking of your lovely stepfamily, how is James doing?"

"Better than expected," Abby said. "He was released from the hospital the day before yesterday."

"You've seen him?"

"No, but I spoke with him briefly on the phone. I went by the house as soon as I arrived in town, but he wasn't up to company."

Brie gave her a look. "Who told you that? Lydia? You're hardly company."

"You can't blame her for being protective," Abby said. "I'd probably do the same in her shoes. Besides, we'll have plenty of time to catch up while I'm here."

"I guess." Brie picked at the food, then walked back to the rail as she sipped her coffee. "I'm just surprised he was released so soon after a major heart attack."

Abby nodded. "I was, too, but Lydia says his doctors are pleased with his progress. He'll have to take it easy, of course, but that's why I'm here."

"Much to the chagrin of your wicked stepsister, I'm sure."

"I'm not a kid anymore. I can handle Lydia."

"Famous last words—" Brie broke off as a boat with an outboard motor puttered up to the dock. She set her cup aside and leaned over the rail to get a better look through the lush vegetation. "Who could that be this early on a Saturday morning? Are you expecting company?"

"No one but you. I doubt anyone else knows I'm around." They watched as a tall, lean man in damp board shorts climbed out of the boat and looped rope lines around the metal cleats bolted into the dock. He was shirtless and bronzed, his longish hair tousled from the wind.

Brie called down to him. "Hey! This is private property in case you didn't notice the sign!"

He turned to stare up at them. After a moment, he lifted a hand and waved.

"I'm not being friendly, dude," Brie muttered. "Don't wave back," she admonished when Abby lifted her hand.

The man removed his sunglasses and tossed them in the boat while simultaneously reaching for a T-shirt he pulled over his head.

"See? You've encouraged him. He's coming up here." Brie sucked in a quick breath. "Oh, hell no."

"What?"

Her gaze narrowed. "Without sunglasses, he looks just like…" Her voice trailed off on a faint gasp. "Oh, my God, it *is* him! You've got to be kidding me!"

Abby turned back to the newcomer. Her stomach fluttered unexpectedly as they made eye contact. It was him all right. *Wade Easton.* Last she'd heard, he left town sometime after she moved to Atlanta. They hadn't spoken in well over a decade. She rarely even thought about him these days, and she only dreamed about him once in a blue moon. After all that time, what was he doing down there on her dock?

And did it really matter? Maybe he'd heard she was back in town and decided to drop by to catch up. Or maybe he wanted to satisfy his curiosity and assuage his guilt at the same time. After all, she was certainly curious about him. First love and all that.

Brie swore under her breath. "You'd think he'd know better than to show his face around here after what he did to you."

"That was a long time ago," Abby said. "We were kids. Everybody gets dumped in high school. It's a rite of passage. I don't hold a grudge."

"Well, you should. Once a cheat, always a cheat in my book," Brie fumed. "Damned if the rat bastard doesn't still look good."

"How dare he!" Abby said with a chuckle, though her heart thudded and her palms had started to sweat. She wiped them on her shorts and hoped Brie hadn't noticed.

"He could have at least had the decency to pack on a few pounds and chop off that hair," Brie said.

But no. He was still lean and cut and bronzed, his thick hair curling at his nape. Abby couldn't tear her gaze away and, apparently, neither could Brie.

"How did he even know you were back?" she asked.

"I have no idea."

Brie's voice dropped accusingly. "Please tell me you're not still in touch with him."

"We haven't spoken in years." Abby's nails dug into her palms. The pain surprised her. She hadn't realized her fingers were clenched so tightly. With an effort, she relaxed her hands and clasped them behind her back as the subject of Brie's contempt left the dock and slowly climbed the flagstones steps, disappearing momentarily into the jungle of vegetation that crowded the stairs. As one, Abby and Brie leaned to the right to try and catch another glimpse of him.

By the time he emerged from the oleanders and palm fronds, Abby had managed to recover her poise. She leaned against a wrought iron post, folded her arms and stared down at him.

He paused on the steps to squint up at them. He wasn't yet thirty, but the crinkles around his eyes and mouth gave him a kind of world-weary air that belied his age, and the way he carried himself seemed guarded. He wasn't the same guy Abby had fallen for in high school. This Wade Easton had seen and done things that had matured and jaded him. The hint of darkness in his eyes only served to make him more attractive.

"Rat bastard," Brie muttered.

Indeed.

He called up to them. "Morning, ladies!"

The voice was deeper and the drawl a little less pronounced now that he'd spent time away from Alabama. Where had he been all these years? Abby wondered.

Not that it was any of her business. Not that she really cared.

She bristled as memories betrayed her. The sight of him slipping through her open bedroom window with knowing eyes and a devastating grin. The utter thrill of their secret and forbidden liaison. Her mother hadn't approved of Wade. Yet another thing that had made him all the more attractive to Abby.

How dare you, Wade Easton! How dare you stand there on my property with that same look in your eyes as if you still know me. As if the past ten years never happened.

Oh, yes, that look…those eyes…

Some things never changed.

She drew a quick breath as she drank him in despite the sudden sting of bitterness at his betrayal. Her mother wasn't the only one who had deserted her that last summer on the lake. In her hour of greatest need, Wade Easton had turned to someone else. *How could you do that to me?*

Abby had sobbed. Such melodrama. The memory made her a little uncomfortable.

Brie moved over to the edge of the terrace and planted a hand on her hip as she glared down at him. "Wade Easton, as I live and breathe."

He tipped his head. "Brianna."

"My friends call me Brie, but for you, Brianna will do just fine."

Abby's gaze remained glued to him. She saw his lips twitch and thought, *You* would *find this whole situation amusing.* She cursed him again as she once more unclenched her fists.

"You've got some nerve showing up here," Brie told him. "After everything you've done?"

He continued up the steps. "Are you referring to the past, or has something a little more immediate put you in a lather?"

"You know what I'm talking about. I shouldn't have to spell it out for you, but I will if you insist. In excruciating detail."

He cocked his head. "Is this about your brother's boat?"

"Let's get something straight right from the get-go." Her voice was like an ice cube sliding down the spine on a cold winter's morning. Abby would not want to face off against Brie Fortier in a legal battle. Or in a dark alley. "My brother's stolen boat is only one of many grievances I have against you. At least in that situation, no one was hurt, although an argument could be made for the financial hardship he's suffered. He'd like nothing more than to put the whole incident behind him and move on, but your company refuses to honor his policy. I shouldn't have to tell you how much that coverage cost him only to have his claim slow-walked by some clerk until the company can find a way to wiggle out of their obligations. Which, if I'm not mistaken, is where you come in."

Wait, what? Abby didn't have a clue what either of them were talking about. And here she'd thought Brie was outraged on her behalf. "What boat?"

They both cut her a glance as if they'd forgotten she was there. Humbling, to say the least.

"Brett's boat was stolen from the marina a couple of weeks ago," Brie explained.

"Not just any boat," Wade said. "A vessel that's worth upward of a quarter of a million dollars."

Abby's mouth dropped. "What was Brett doing with a boat like that?"

The question seemed to irritate Brie. "Why does it matter? That's his business. What matters is that the boat was fully covered by a 'reputable' company," she said with air quotes. "However, despite his account being current, they refuse to honor his claim."

"That's not exactly true," Wade said. "They haven't honored the claim yet. The company isn't obligated to cut him a check until a thorough investigation has been conducted."

"The police have already investigated," Brie said.

"No, the police wrote a report," Wade countered.

"Which should be all that is needed to process his claim."

"You're a lawyer," Wade said. "You know that's not how it works."

Brie lifted her chin. "We'll see you in court if we have to."

He shrugged. "No skin off my teeth, but you should know Global Alliance has deep pockets. If you decide to sue, they could drag this out for years. Besides all that, I'd recommend you run any legal action by your brother before you commit. I have a feeling the last thing he'll want is more scrutiny."

"Meaning?"

"Ask him," Wade said. "But this whole conversation is beside the point. I'm not here to argue about a missing boat. I came to see Abby."

"What about?" Brie demanded.

"That's between Abby and me."

The whole confrontation seemed surreal to Abby. Just a few short days ago, she'd been in Atlanta enjoying a lucrative career in commercial real estate. She had a great job, a lovely condo and a busy social life. Now here she was back in her hometown, back on the lake, listening to an argument between the two people she'd once been the closest to. Their current conflict was like the worst kind of déjà vu. The two had never gotten along.

"This is unreal," she murmured.

Brie frowned. "What is?"

"The way you two are going at it. It's like we never left high school." She fixed her gaze on Wade. "Anything you have to say to me you can say in front of Brie." She remained at the rail, keeping the wrought iron barrier between them. She didn't know why, but putting an obstacle in front of Wade Easton made her feel better.

Now who's acting like she's still in high school?

Wade gave her the strangest look, as if the same thought had crossed his mind.

"I'd prefer to speak in private," he said. "I won't take much of your time."

Brie moved to Abby's side, turning her back on Wade as she lowered her voice. "Do you believe this guy? Showing up out of the blue after all these years, insisting on being alone with you. I don't feel comfortable with that. He'll probably try to grill you about Brett."

"But I don't know anything about Brett and his boat," Abby said.

"That won't stop him. He's obviously up to something."

"You think everyone has an ulterior motive," Abby reminded her.

"Because they almost always do."

"Maybe." Abby glanced down at Wade. "It won't hurt to hear what he has to say."

"It might," Brie said with a glance over her shoulder. "It might hurt a lot."

"I'm not worried. Besides, it's a beautiful Saturday morning and you must have a million things to do on your day off. Go on. I'll be fine. I'll call you later."

"Are you sure?"

"Yes, absolutely."

Brie nodded. "If you say so. Just don't let him get to you, okay? Wade Easton has always been your kryptonite."

"When we were teenagers, maybe. Not anymore."

Brie didn't sound so certain. "Look at him. He's still—"

"I know."

"Call me as soon as he leaves. I'd like to hear what he has to say for himself these days. Plus, I want to make sure you're all right."

"Now you're just being melodramatic," Abby scolded. "It's not as if he intends to murder me in broad daylight."

"You never know." Brie gave Wade one final warning glare before exiting through the French doors and pulling them closed behind her.

A long silence ensued. Wade finally said, "That wasn't at all awkward."

Abby gave him a tight smile. "Not one bit." She tried to sound casually indifferent. "Do you want to come up or shall I come down?"

"I'll come to you."

Four loaded words if she'd ever heard any.

She took an unconscious step back as Wade bounded up the stairs. And then he was right in front of her, and she instantly regretted the invitation. She shouldn't have allowed him to come up to her private space. They were standing much too close in the intimate environment of her terrace. She could see the faint shadow of a beard on his lower face and a gleam of uncertainty in his eyes.

And behind that uncertainty was a flicker of something dark and troubling, something that sent a sharp chill straight through her heart.

Chapter Two

Disquiet settled over Abby like a dark cloud. Wade Easton obviously hadn't come to apologize for his past behavior or make amends for an old betrayal. Foolish of her to entertain such a notion. No, something more immediate had brought him to her doorstep, but she couldn't imagine what that something was.

In the split second before either of them said anything, she ran through a litany of troubling possibilities as one had a tendency to do under such circumstances. Her first thought was that something had happened to her grandmother, but they'd video-chatted earlier before Brie arrived, and everything had been fine. And, anyway, how would Wade know something about her grandmother that she didn't?

No, this wasn't about her family. Abby told herself she could relax on that front. Her stepfather was the only one with health issues at the moment, and if he'd suffered a setback or another attack, her stepsister would have called. Lydia herself appeared to be the picture of health, and Wade didn't know any of her other relatives. As for close friends, Brie was the only person she'd remained close to in Fairhope, so it didn't seem likely that Wade was here to impart bad news.

Then why the dark look in his eyes? Why that shiver of dread down her spine?

Maybe Brie was right. Maybe he'd come here hoping to uncover more information about her brother's stolen boat. That would explain why he refused to speak in front of Brie. He knew she'd run straight to Brett. But if he thought Abby could help him—or would help him—he was sorely mistaken. She had no particular affinity or allegiance to Brett Fortier, but Brie was a different matter. Abby would never do anything to hurt the one friend who had stuck by her during the hard times, who had been nothing but kind and loyal to her throughout the years. Brie had been there for her when Wade Easton had bolted. Abby strongly believed in letting bygones be bygones, but some lessons couldn't be unlearned.

All this flashed through her mind as she and Wade silently took the other's measure. She was suddenly all too aware of her bare face and windblown hair. Not exactly the look she would have chosen had she anticipated an encounter with an old boyfriend. She reminded herself that he was casual and windblown, too, but on him, it looked good.

She finally found her voice and a hint of defiance. "If this is about Brett Fortier, I'm afraid you're wasting your time. I don't know anything about a stolen boat."

"It's not about Brett. At least not directly."

She frowned. "Then why are you here?"

He seemed oddly at a loss. "At the moment, damned if I know. It seemed like a good idea at the time. I thought I owed you, but now I realize it wasn't my place to come here. I didn't stop to think that I might be the last person you'd want to see."

Well, that did nothing to clarify his intentions.

Abby shrugged. "I wouldn't go that far, but you do owe me an explanation. It's been over ten years since we spoke, and our last conversation was hardly amicable."

"I remember."

She shivered at the unexpected note of regret in his voice. "Then you'll forgive me if I'm a little thrown by your sudden appearance."

"Yeah, I get it. I feel a little off-kilter myself."

Off-kilter? Wade Easton? She found that hard to believe. "Let's start with an easy question then. How did you even know where to find me?"

"I heard you were back in town. I took the chance you'd be here." He glanced around the sun-dappled terrace. "You always loved this cottage. So much so that you hated having strangers rent it every summer. You planned to buy it from your mother as soon as you were able so that no one but you could ever set foot in it again."

Her heart flip-flopped. "Good grief. You remember all that?"

He gave her a brief smile. "I remember a lot of things. Ten years isn't that long."

"More than ten. And it seems like a lifetime."

"Not to me." His gaze came back to her and seemed to deepen, making her even more curious about the reason for his visit. Curious and wary. Yet for some strange reason, she hesitated to press him on his motive. Call it a premonition, call it being a coward, but she wanted to hide for as long as she could behind the banality of their reunion.

"How long have you been back?" he asked as if sensing her reluctance.

"A day or so. And you?"

"A little longer. I'm here on business."

"Yes, I gathered that. Is that why you were out on the water so early?" Something suddenly occurred to her and she said anxiously, "Wait. Does this have something to do with all the sirens we heard? Has there been an accident? Is that why you didn't want to speak in front of Brie? Has something happened to Brett?"

"He's fine as far as I know. I haven't seen him in years. As to why I went out early, I took the boat as far north as the old bridge to go diving."

She said in surprise, "Scuba diving? Why?"

He paused. "It seemed like another good idea at the time."

His equivocation only fed the awkwardness and her nervousness. Maybe he really had come here to apologize, but his pride wouldn't allow him to come right out and say so.

Buy why now? Why so mysterious?

She tried to gauge his expression as she continued to quiz him. "Why would you go all the way up there to dive? There can't be much to see. The bridge was demolished years ago after the county declared it unsafe for traffic. They tried barricades, but people just knocked them down or drove around them. I guess they thought they had no choice but to tear the whole thing down before someone got hurt. Some of the iron was salvaged, but the rest…" She shrugged, realizing she had imparted more information about the old bridge than he or anyone else would ever want to know. Nerves did that to her. "I'm told it was quite a site, all those heavy girders crashing into the water."

"There's still a lot of debris on the lakebed," he said. "Not exactly an environmentally friendly demolition. I guess no one cares about that end of the lake. The old money has always been on the southern end. New money, too, judging by all the houses going up around here."

Abby turned her back on the water, leaning

against one of the posts as she faced him. "What were you diving for?"

He gave her a look. "I would have thought that obvious. I was hoping to find Brett Fortier's missing speedboat."

"So this *is* about his boat." Abby didn't know whether to be relieved or aggravated. It wasn't that she wanted or expected an apology after all this time, but an acknowledgement of his past bad behavior might have been nice. That earlier flicker of regret was likely all she'd get. "Well? What is it you think I know?"

"I told you, I'm not here about the boat."

"But you just said—"

"I said I was hoping to find it at the bottom of the lake. One of my aerial photographs indicated a shadow about forty feet down that didn't appear to be bridge debris. I thought it worth a closer look."

"I don't get it. Why would someone steal an expensive boat just to sink it?"

"Maybe they were after something onboard," he said.

"Such as?"

"Something illegal would be my guess."

She gave him a knowing scrutiny. "You think Brett sunk his own boat, don't you?"

Wade stared back without flinching. "We both know he's capable."

"People can change."

"Some can. Most don't."

"Including you?" She immediately regretted the question. Not because she wanted to spare his feelings but because it revealed a little too much of hers.

"I'm probably not the best person to answer that question," he said.

There was that look again. The old simmering intensity. Maybe Brie had been right to warn her. Wade Easton was still a dangerous man. Abby had a feeling he'd been a lot of women's kryptonite over the years.

"Do you think Brett's changed?" he asked.

"I don't know. I try to give everyone the benefit of the doubt. I admit, though, that I was surprised to hear he owned a boat worth a quarter of a million dollars. That's a lot of money, especially considering I don't even know what he does for a living. Brie's always been a little evasive when it comes to her brother."

"Probably with good reason. My question isn't why he bought an expensive boat," Wade said. "Brett Fortier has always been attracted to glittery things. What I'd like to know is why he needed one with that kind of power and speed."

"Brie says he's an adrenaline junkie."

"That's one explanation."

"And another?"

"Maybe he needed to outrun someone down

south. Gun runners, drug traffickers, the Coast Guard."

"That's wild speculation unless you know something I don't." When he merely shrugged, Abby said, "For someone who didn't come here to talk about Brett Fortier, you seem to spend a lot of time and energy on him."

"And here I thought I was just answering your questions."

The conversation still seemed surreal to Abby. It was disconcerting to discover that Wade Easton could still throw her off-balance. But she reminded herself she wasn't an infatuated teenager anymore. She knew how to protect herself. She unfolded her arms and visibly straightened from the post as if to prove that point.

"Okay. I have another question for you," she said. "There was always bad blood between you and Brett. You two couldn't stand each other in high school. Is it possible you *want* to believe the worst about him? Maybe this isn't so much about a stolen boat as it is your desire to take him down a peg or two."

He looked annoyed. "Believe it or not, I haven't given Brett Fortier more than a passing thought since high school. I'm here to do a job. Nothing more, nothing less."

"What exactly is your job?"

"In a nutshell, I'm paid to find expensive things that have gone missing."

That his smile could still make her pulse race was extremely irritating to Abby. She felt the need to take *him* down a peg or two, which was also irritating and not in the least admirable, but human. Or so she told herself.

"I gathered from your discussion with Brie that you work for an insurance company."

"Not exclusively. I'm not on any company's payroll except my own."

"Still, it's not quite what I would have expected of you."

"Just out of curiosity, what did you expect from me?"

She took a moment to answer. "I guess I thought you'd eventually go into law enforcement like your dad. You used to talk about it sometimes."

"I did consider it."

"But?"

"It wasn't the right fit. I like solving mysteries, but I also like making money." He glanced back at her. "Anything wrong with that?"

"I'm probably not the right person to answer *that* question," she said. "I've spent most of my professional life chasing the next big sale."

"And yet here you are back on Shutter Lake."

"Temporarily." The awkwardness had evaporated, and their chat had become almost congenial. Not good. She'd let her guard drop, and that was a very dangerous situation when it came to Wade Easton. She'd found that out the hard way.

"I heard about your stepfather," he said. "I assume that's why you're here. Frankly, I'm surprised you didn't come back a long time ago to run your mom's business."

"They've managed fine without me until now, but this is the busy season, and Lydia has her hands full. I'm here to help in any way I can."

"I'm sure your efforts will be appreciated."

She couldn't tell if he was being sarcastic or not. Did he remember Lydia's attitude back in the day? Maybe he thought she'd changed over the years. Abby still harbored that faint hope herself, but leopards rarely changed their spots. She would do well to remember that when it came to her stepsister and to her ex-boyfriend.

"What did your grandmother think about the move?" he asked. "As I recall, she couldn't wait to get you out of this town."

"To be perfectly honest, she wasn't thrilled," Abby said. "Not that I blame her. This place holds a lot of bad memories for her. For both of us."

"For all of us."

Something in his voice brought another shiver to her spine. His eyes had taken on a faraway look as if he'd drifted a million miles away. Was he thinking about that last summer? Was he sorry for the way things had ended between them? Doubtful. He'd moved on long before she had.

Despite her insistence earlier that she didn't hold a grudge, she felt an unpleasant sting of the old resentment, chased by the burn of lingering humiliation. Everyone in town had known about his betrayal before she did. She could tell herself a million times over that what happened back then no longer mattered. Kids did foolish, regrettable things to one another in high school.

But it had taken her a long time to get over Wade Easton. Longer still to rebuild her confidence and ability to trust, his betrayal coming as it had on the heels of her mother's abandonment. Maybe under normal circumstances, she could have eventually put their breakup into perspective. Maybe even laughed about it in time. But being discarded by her mother *and* her first love was a double blow that had taken a toll. Not that she would ever let on to Wade or anyone else how much pain he'd caused her.

He moved to the rail and stared out over the lake. She wanted to ask him to leave, but she didn't. Instead, she studied his profile as he squinted into the sun. Strange how everything about him seemed so familiar, and yet she really didn't know anything about him.

If her scrutiny bothered him, he didn't let on. "The water is always like glass in this cove. You could travel anywhere in the world and be hard-pressed to beat this view."

Reluctantly, she turned her gaze to the scenery.

"I never get tired of it," she said. "I enjoy my life in the city, but there's something magical about this place. The way the sunlight dances across the surface of the water…the play of shadows along the banks. Sometimes it almost seems too beautiful to be real."

"I prefer it by moonlight." His voice dropped intimately. "The water has a different vibe at night. Mysterious. Seductive. A little dangerous."

Like you.

His gaze was still on the water. "I rented this cottage for a few weeks one summer. Did Lydia tell you?"

"She never mentioned it." Abby's family had at least a dozen rental properties on the lake. The valuable real estate made up the bulk of the company's assets. She'd long ago become accustomed to strangers coming and going from those houses, but the image of Wade Easton sitting on her terrace, cooking in her kitchen, sleeping in her bed jolted her.

"My mother wasn't well," he said. "Like you, I came back home to lend a hand. The cottage happened to be available, so I signed a short-term lease."

Abby moved up beside him at the rail. "I didn't know. About your mother, I mean."

"Not many people did. Dad's very protective of her privacy. And his, too, I guess. He was still the police chief back then, and you know how people around here like to gossip. My mother has always suffered from clinical depression, but that summer, she had a complete breakdown. Her doctor recommended she be admitted to a mental health facility in Mobile. She was there for nearly two weeks."

"I had no idea." Abby resisted the urge to put her hand over his. "How is she now?"

"Good days and bad. If she takes her medication, more good than bad."

"And your dad?"

"He took early retirement to spend more time with her. Leaving the police department was a difficult decision for him. Being a cop was all he ever knew. He still consults on certain cases, but the past few years haven't been easy for him. He's not the same man he used to be."

"It's hard when they get older," Abby murmured.

He turned to stare down at her. "It's harder when they don't."

WADE REGRETTED NOT telling her the real reason for his visit as soon as they were alone. Revealing his discovery was proving more difficult with each passing second. But just blurting out the truth seemed wrong. Especially considering how they'd left things the last time they spoke. He wanted to believe that she'd forgiven if not forgotten, but that tiny glimmer of contempt in her eyes as she'd stared down at him from the terrace had quickly disabused him of that notion. Given the awkwardness of their first meeting, he'd felt the need to ease into his revelation.

At least, that's what he told himself. But maybe his reluctance wasn't quite so altruistic. Maybe he'd wanted to spend a few minutes in her company before he had to watch the horror of his discovery dawn in her eyes.

"Wade? Are you okay?"

He turned with a frown. "What?"

"You seemed a million miles away just now."

"I guess I was there for a minute." His fingers tightened around the wrought iron railing. The hint of huskiness in her voice had always had a powerful impact on him. That he still found her incredibly attractive was a little disconcerting. The pretty girl he'd known in high school had turned into a real knockout of a woman. The sprinkle of freckles across her bare face and the windblown tangles at her temples only added to her appeal.

"Are you worried about your mom? You said she's okay if she takes her medication, right?"

"It's not that. I mean, I'm always a little worried about her," he admitted. "But she was fine the last time we talked."

"Then what is it?"

He turned to meet her quizzical gaze. "I should

have told you right from the start. There's no easy way to say this."

"Then just say it. Your evasiveness is making me nervous."

"I found something at the bottom of the lake."

She tucked back a strand of loose hair. "Not the boat?"

"No. Not the boat. A car." He glanced away, dreading what he still had to disclose. "I think it's been down there since before the bridge was demolished."

"Okay, you found a car. Why is this information I need to know?"

"It's not just any car." His hesitation was so slight he wondered if she noticed. "It's what's left of a Rolls Royce Wraith."

She said in confusion, "I don't understand—" Then she broke off on a gasp. "Wait. You don't think it's Mother's car."

He met her gaze with another nod.

"But…it can't be. She left town in that car years ago."

"We all thought she did. But have you ever known anyone else around here to drive a Rolls Royce? That's not a car you forget."

Her response was a little too quick, as if she desperately wanted to prove him wrong before the conversation went any further. "No, but I've been gone from the area for over ten years. So have you. Neither of us can possibly know all the cars that have come and gone during that time. And, yes, I imagine a Rolls Royce is still an uncommon sight in these parts, but I saw plenty of other expensive vehicles in town when I drove through." She gave a vague wave toward the water. "Look at all the multi-million-dollar homes that have been built on the lake in the past few years. People with that kind of money have a tendency to own expensive cars and boats. I'm telling you that's not my mother's car."

Wade hoped she was right, but deep down, he already knew that she wasn't. "If a vehicle like that had ended up in the lake by accident or otherwise, word would have gotten out. A car of that caliber doesn't go missing without someone noticing."

"Maybe someone did notice. Maybe a police report was filed. How would either of us know since we didn't live here?"

Wade tried to keep his tone even. He didn't want to upset her, but she needed to be prepared for the reality of his discovery. "My dad would have mentioned it. He was the police chief until just a few years ago. I'm willing to bet the car's been down there longer than he's been retired."

"Then ask him," she said. "Or don't. It should be easy enough to prove ownership by checking the registration."

"That might not be as easy as you think," Wade said. "Both front and rear license plates are missing. Maybe they disintegrated from pressure and corrosion or maybe they were removed before the car went into the lake. We've no way of knowing. The body of the vehicle is badly rusted. The police may be able to uncover a VIN etching once the car is brought up, but lifting a vehicle from forty feet of water is no easy feat. They'll have to bring in a special crane and possibly a barge if there's no access from the bank. It could take days to get the equipment in place."

Her expression remained a mixture of confusion, disbelief and maybe already a hint of dread as she stared at him in silence. "Why would the police go to that kind of effort and expense to raise an abandoned car? There must be dozens of them up and down the lake."

"I don't know about dozens, but likely a few," he said. "However, this particular car is a crime scene."

He saw her take a breath. "What do you mean?" When he hesitated, she said, "Just tell me. Don't drag this out any longer than necessary."

"Human remains are inside the car. Someone was handcuffed to the steering wheel before the vehicle went over the bridge."

Her hand flew to her mouth.

"I'm sorry," he said.

"Don't say that." She sounded almost angry. "Not yet. This may not be what you seem to think it is. It's possible you're mistaken about the make and model. What about the color?"

"The paint is too badly corroded to know for certain."

"Then how can you be so sure?"

"I just am."

Her eyes glittered. "That's not good enough. Did you even think to look for splotches of paint? How thoroughly could you have examined the car underwater?"

"I know what I saw."

"You personally saw—"

"Yes."

She squeezed her eyes closed as the color leeched from her face, highlighting the dusting of freckles across her nose and cheekbones. "This is horrible. Like something from a nightmare. The images I have in my head…" She shuddered and then seemed to shake herself as if once again gathering her resolve. "But it's not Mother's car down there. It's not my mother inside."

He gentled his tone. "I could be wrong, but I don't think I am. Let's just think about it for a minute. Aside from the make and model of the vehicle, the timing makes sense. The car's been in the water since before the bridge was demolished. Did you ever see or hear from your mother after she left town that night?"

Her eyes fluttered closed again as her fingers curled around the railing. "No, but that's the way she wanted it. She told me not to come looking for her. She said she wanted a new life without family expectations. Without me."

Without me. Still so much hurt in those two words. He wondered how she'd coped with the pain of her mother's desertion all these years. Had she been able to put it into perspective without blaming herself as so many abandoned kids had a tendency to do? He liked to think she'd gotten on with her life after she left Fairhope. He wanted to believe she'd been happy in Atlanta. Without him.

He resisted the urge to brush back her hair, but such an intimate gesture wouldn't be appropriate or welcome. It might only serve to remind her of *his* betrayal. Instead, he said, "Once the car is brought up, the medical examiner can compare dental records or run a DNA analysis to determine the victim's identity. Then we'll know for sure."

She said nothing for the longest moment. Then softly, "Supposing it is her…what do you think happened?"

"I don't know."

"It just doesn't seem possible. For so long, I thought—" She broke off as she glanced out over the water. "The note she left on my dresser was handwritten. No one could have faked it. In the days leading up to her departure, she made a lot of complex business maneuvers. She shuffled money around, signed contracts and agreements so the company would run smoothly in her absence, saw to it that I would be taken care of financially. All of that took planning and coordination with lawyers and advisors. None of those arrangements could have been done overnight. Then she withdrew a bundle of cash, packed her suitcases and left town. I never heard from her again."

Wade nodded, but said nothing.

"Over the years, there have been sightings," she said. "A friend or acquaintance would swear they spotted her in Spain or Italy or somewhere in South America, and Grandmother would hire yet another private detective. Nothing ever panned out, but those sightings were enough to convince us that she was alive and well and living the life she wanted."

"Do you still have the note?"

"Yes, somewhere."

"What else did it say? The gist."

"'I know you won't understand what I'm about to do, and you may even despise me for it, but I hope in time you'll regard my decision in a kinder light. You're an adult now. You'll be going away to college soon and starting your own life, so I feel this is my time to be selfish. I've been unhappy for so very long. My marriage to James was a mistake. He's a good man, but he's not the right man for me. I've fallen in love with someone else. Deeply in love. The kind of love that comes around once in a lifetime if you're lucky. It's all very new and fragile, and we need time to ourselves far away from Shutter Lake, far away from work responsibilities and family obligations. Please know this is what I want. This is what I need. Don't come looking for me. Let me have my moment in the sun. When the time is right, I'll be in touch. Love, Mother.'"

Not just the gist but verbatim, he suspected. He wondered how many times she'd read that note over the years. How many times she'd wondered how her own mother could have abandoned her so easily and seemingly without an ounce of remorse.

She'd been staring out over the water as she recited the message, but now she turned to him, doubt flickering in her eyes. "Wade. You don't think that was a suicide note, do you?"

"Why would she pack her bags and withdraw a large amount of cash just to drive her car over the side of the bridge? Not to mention that the victim was handcuffed to the steering wheel."

"Someone did that to her. That's what you're saying. My mother was murdered." The color had come back into her cheeks, but she still looked shaken. Who wouldn't be?

"We'll know more when they bring up the car," he said.

She ran a hand up and down her arm. "The day after she left, I had the strangest feeling that something was wrong. I wouldn't call it a premonition or even intuition. Eventually, I decided it was just my way of coping. I didn't want to believe she could leave me so easily. Without even saying goodbye. I even entertained the notion for a while that she'd been kidnapped. I imagined all kinds of scenarios, anything but the reality of her callous abandonment. I even took the note to the police station and refused to leave until I'd spoken with your dad."

"I didn't know that," Wade said in surprise. "He never told me."

"He probably wanted to protect my privacy. He kindly and gently explained to me that there was nothing he could do. By every indication, my mother had left town of her own accord. The note and the financial arrangements appeared to be well thought out by someone in full charge of her faculties. Under the circumstances, his hands were tied, he said. I later learned that he did make inquiries. He talked to my mother's attorney and business advisor, and he spoke with my stepfather at length. I guess he was satisfied by what he heard. I certainly never suspected anything was amiss."

"Why would you if everything in that note was true? I think she meant every word of it. She planned to leave town and start a new life, but someone stopped her."

"But who?" Abby's voice was still hushed, her eyes haunted.

"Someone with a powerful motive."

"After all this time…after all the terrible things I've thought about her over the years…"

"You're not responsible for any of this," Wade said. "Don't get tangled up in misplaced guilt."

She nodded. "You're right. We don't know anything yet. There's a chance you could be mistaken about the car. But I still need talk to my grandmother. I can't let her hear about this from someone else."

"I don't think that's a good idea," Wade said. "This is a homicide investigation now. You need to let the police handle the notifications. I shouldn't even be here."

"But you came because you thought I should know. You said yourself it could take days to recover the car. Once they bring in heavy equipment, people are bound to talk. The operation may even make the local news. I can't let Grandmother find out that way. She'd be devastated."

He conceded her point. "You're right. You should go tell her in person so long as you both understand the need for discretion. Maybe it's for the best. You can stay in Atlanta until things get sorted out down here."

She bit her lip, deep in thought. "What about

James? He's still legally her husband. Doesn't he have a right to know?"

Wade said carefully, "I wouldn't talk to James under any circumstances."

"But—"

"Abby, think. The spouse is always a prime suspect."

Her eyes widened in horror.

"I'm not saying he did anything wrong," Wade rushed to clarify. "But the police may want to observe his demeanor when they break the news to him."

She folded her arms and hugged them to her middle. "This is silly. James would never have done anything to hurt my mother. He was wildly in love with her."

"Which gives him a pretty powerful motive if he suspected she was leaving him for another man. Jealousy can make people lose all reason. Maybe he confronted her and things got out of hand. There's also the financial angle to consider. The company belonged to your mother. He stood to lose almost everything if she divorced him."

"But she left him in charge."

"For how long? Until you were old enough to take over?"

"I guess that makes me a suspect as well," she said. "Unless Mother changed her will at the last minute, I'm the one who stood to benefit the most from her death. We didn't exactly have the best relationship that summer. Our arguments got pretty heated at times. She didn't approve of my clothes, my friends. You…" She glanced at him. "She tried to break us up. Did you know that?"

"I guess that gives me a motive, too."

"I don't know about that. You did a pretty good job of ending our relationship all by yourself."

He'd wondered when they would get around to talking about that. "Things weren't always what they seemed that summer."

Her gaze was very direct. "It seemed pretty clear to me."

"Two sides to every story," he said. "But maybe now isn't the best time to get into all that."

"On that we agree."

"When will you go back to Atlanta?"

"Today. I'll spend the night with my grand-mother and drive back tomorrow."

He frowned at that. "I thought we agreed you'd stay in the city for a few days."

"I never agreed to that. I want to be here when the car is recovered. The medical examiner may need a sample of my DNA."

"You don't have to be in town for that."

She frowned right back at him. "Why don't you want me here? What is it you're not telling me?"

"It's not a matter of what I want," he said. "You'll be safer in Atlanta."

"Safe from what?"

"Safe from your mother's killer," he said bluntly. "Don't you get it? Your inheritance not only makes you a suspect. It may also make you a target."

Chapter Three

After leaving Abby's place, Wade took the boat back north. The temperature had risen by mid-morning, and the lake was already teeming with speedboats and Jet Skis and the occasional para-sailer gliding by overhead. The weekend crowd had descended with a vengeance. Kids splashed and shrieked in the shallows as parents watched from loungers on the bank or floated nearby on inner tubes and air mattresses.

The incessant thrum of engines took Wade back to his younger days when he and his friends would hit the water as soon as they got off work from whatever job they'd managed to snag for the summer. Shutter Lake had been a great place to grow up, but the area was changing. The water toys were getting bigger and faster, and the houses perched atop the embankments more imposing. The crime that had always festered in the shadows had started to creep out into the sunlight.

He waited until he was well away from the traffic before he opened the throttle and stood behind the wheel so that he could enjoy the wind on his face. When he was within sight of the bridge ruins, he reduced his speed and lifted his binoculars. Several uniformed officers milled about on the bank waiting for the divers to surface. Two lake patrol vessels guarded the area from either direction, so he didn't try to approach.

Maneuvering toward the bank, he cut the engine and allowed the boat to drift underneath trailing willow branches. He wasn't trying to hide, but he had no wish to be seen. The last thing he wanted was to be tied up at the police station answering an endless stream of questions. He'd already given his statement to the first officer who had arrived on the scene after his call and then a little while later to a detective. If they needed to talk to him again, they had his number. Meanwhile, he had things to do, places to go, people to see. A missing speedboat to find. If he happened to flush out a murderer in the process, so much the better.

He told himself this was not his fight. He had no business getting tangled up in a homicide investigation. He'd done his due diligence by notifying the authorities and breaking the news to Abby. Anything else would just be meddling.

But finding Eva McRae's car at the bottom of the lake after all this time intrigued him. Gnawed at him. A murderer had been walking the streets of his hometown for ten long years, smug in the knowledge that he or she had committed the perfect crime and gotten away with it. Or had guilt slowly been eating away at the killer?

He listened to the water sloshing against the hull and thought about the night Eva had supposedly left town. He and Abby had taken his old boat out for a late-night cruise. They'd drifted for hours under the stars, listening to music while they talked and kissed. They were late getting back home. He half-expected to find every light in the house blazing and a furious Eva waiting for them on the veranda. Instead, the place was dark and quiet. Looking back now, the silence seemed portentous. According to Abby, she'd gone straight up to her room, but she hadn't found the note propped on her dresser until the following morning. The assumption had always been that Eva had left the house sometime later, well after midnight. But if Abby hadn't turned on her bedroom light, she wouldn't have noticed the note. Eva might have already been gone by the time he'd dropped Abby at the house. Her car might have been pushed off the bridge while the two of them had been floating under the stars.

Murdered. In cold blood.

The images forming inside his head were bone-chilling. It was entirely possible Eva had still been alive and conscious when the car had gone over the bridge. He could imagine her panic when she hit the water, the absolute terror she must have felt as the vehicle sank. The killer would have watched from the bridge until the car was out of sight.

As the son of a cop, Wade had learned a thing or two about murder investigations. The first and likeliest suspect was almost always the spouse. James McRae certainly had means, motive and opportunity, but Eva had made a lot of enemies in her day. Ruthless and savvy, she'd built a small empire by snatching up foreclosures and acquiring properties along the lake at rock bottom prices. She hadn't been shy about taking advantage of misery and misfortune. Any number of people could have wanted her dead. Vengeance as a motive was right up there with greed and jealousy.

And then there was the mystery man with whom she'd planned to leave town. No one had ever figured out his identity, though at one time Wade thought he might have known. Nothing concrete, but a very strong hunch that still bedeviled him on occasion.

Wouldn't hurt to make a few inquiries, he decided. Discreetly, of course. Nothing that would draw attention or arouse suspicion.

He continued to monitor the activity through his binoculars. One of the divers surfaced, followed by his partner a few minutes later. They were helped into a boat where they immediately began to shed their gear. Wade was too far away to hear voices, and he'd never mastered the ability to read lips. However, he could tell from their expressions and gestures that they'd witnessed the same grim tableau as he had. They would have photographed and recorded the scene as best they could with underwater equipment, but the car wouldn't have been touched and the remains inside left undisturbed. A crime scene that had been on the lakebed for over a decade would yield little in the way of trace evidence, but precautions would need to be taken nonetheless.

The divers' boat turned and headed south, back toward town and the police station. Several of the cops stationed on the bank climbed back up to their cars. As the engines faded in the distance, an unnerving silence settled over the water. Forty feet down, a murder victim waited for justice.

Wade lowered the binoculars and glanced around. Sunlight reflecting off the water was almost too bright, but he drifted in deep shade. He knew it was his imagination, but the gloom had started to seem unnatural somehow, as if Eva McRae's ghost had floated to the surface and hovered over his boat, watching and waiting and accusing. *You know, don't you? You've always known.*

He wasn't a superstitious person, but the sensation of being watched grew so strong he lifted a hand to rub at the chill bumps on his nape. Maybe he wasn't being stalked by Eva's ghost but by her flesh-and-blood killer. He scanned the trees along the bank, searching for the telltale rustle of branches. Even the birds had gone silent.

Grabbing the binoculars, he searched the opposite shoreline. One of the patrol boats remained in the area, along with a couple of cops on the bank. Wade wondered how they planned to secure the crime scene for the rest of the day and night. Maybe they were counting on secrecy until arrangements could be made to bring up the car, but discretion only lasted so long in a small town. Maybe word had already gotten out, and a few gawkers had made their way to the area to satisfy their curiosity. That would explain the uneasiness he couldn't seem to shake.

He skimmed the banks for several more minutes, then started the engine and guided the boat back into deeper water, waiting until he was out of sight from the lake patrol before he opened the throttle and headed back the way he'd come. Traffic on the water picked up as the lake widened. Veering to the right, he reduced speed as he entered a no-wake zone along a narrow canal where small houses on stilts lined both banks. He pulled up to a private dock and shut off the engine, letting the boat bounce gently off the bumpers. Lifting his hand to shade his eyes, he surveyed the small house perched atop the embankment.

His dad, Sam, sat on the deck drinking coffee and reading a newspaper. When he heard the engine, he folded the paper and set it aside as he watched Wade climb out of the boat and tie off. Neither of them waved or called out. Wade fiddled with the ropes for another long moment before he started up the wooden steps.

"Well, look what the cat dragged up," his dad teased as he picked up a napkin and scrubbed at the traces of ink left on his fingertips from the newsprint.

Wade nodded toward the fluttering pages as he moved into the shade of the covered deck and half-heartedly returned his dad's greeting. The good-natured ribbing made him uncomfortable given the nature of his visit. "You do know you can get the same information online these days. It's called the internet, old-timer. You should look into it."

His dad shrugged. "I like the feel of a real newspaper between my fingers. Besides, a few ink smudges never hurt anyone."

"Can't teach an old dog new tricks, I guess."

"That all depends."

At fifty-nine, his dad was still fit and trim, his posture ramrod straight, but his hair got a little grayer with each passing year, and the lines around his eyes and mouth had deepened since his retirement. He was still a vital guy. Passing time reading and fishing didn't suit him.

"I heard you'd been spotted in town a couple

days ago," he said. "I wondered when you'd get around to stopping by."

"This isn't a pleasure trip," Wade said. "I'm here working a case."

"I heard that, too." His dad continued to scrub at his fingers, then gave up and tossed the napkin aside. "Something about a stolen boat. The insurance company must smell something fishy if they sent you down here."

His dad could play coy all he wanted, but Wade figured he'd already gotten the lowdown from his buddies at the station. He would know all about Wade's meeting with the detective in Major Crimes and his request for a copy of any supporting documents that had been added to the initial police report.

He glanced around the cozy deck. A ceiling fan rotated overhead, stirring his mother's potted ferns while her old tomcat snoozed on one of the rockers. The back door was open, but the shadows were too deep to glimpse anything or anyone through the screen.

"Is Mom around?" he asked in what he hoped was a casual tone.

"She's sleeping in this morning."

Wade frowned. "Kind of late for her, isn't it? Everything okay?"

"Everything is fine. She's painting again and you know how she gets. Loses all track of time. Barely even remembers to eat."

"I'm glad to hear she's painting," Wade said. "Art has always been therapeutic for her."

"Sometimes I worry she's a little too obsessive about it. She'll stay up until all hours when she gets going on a piece she likes. Says she enjoys the quiet. Says she's more creative when it's dark outside. Me? I'm in bed by nine, ten at the latest. But she seems happy, so I don't complain." He shuffled some things around on the table and motioned for Wade to sit. "You want some breakfast?"

"I'm good, thanks."

"Coffee?"

"Maybe in a minute." Instead of sitting at the table, he leaned against the deck railing, his back to the water.

"How long can you stay?"

"Depends on what I find out, but a few more days, at least."

"I meant right now. Should I go wake your mother?"

"No, let her sleep. If I don't catch her this morning, I'll come back in a day or two."

His dad gave him a measured look. "Easy for you to say, but it's my hide on the line if I let you leave before she sees you."

"Actually, I was hoping to have a word with you in private."

His dad squinted up at him. "About Brett Fortier's stolen boat? I doubt I can be of much help, but I'm happy to listen."

"Oh, come on," Wade said. "You're not fooling me with that out-of-the-loop routine. I know how your pipeline works. You probably know more about the case than the detective in charge. More than me, too, for that matter." Wade decided to take a seat after all. He settled across the table from Sam and stretched out his legs. "What's the unofficial consensus?"

"As far as I know, there hasn't been a lot of progress on the case," Sam said. "Nothing substantial has turned up, no concrete evidence, no fingerprints or fibers, no eye-witness accounts. The boat was stolen from the marina a few days after Brett Fortier brought it up from the Gulf. The nearest security camera wasn't working, and the guard had started his rounds on the other side of the marina when it happened. In other words, no one saw or heard anything."

"Do you think it could have been an inside job?" Wade asked.

"Someone working at the marina, you mean?" Sam shrugged. "That's always a possibility, although the guard on duty that night is an ex-cop. I know him. Good man. I don't see him being involved. One of the other employees, who knows? The thieves were in and out quickly, and they knew the guard's rotation, knew which camera to disable. Boats with that kind of price tag come with safeguards. It's not easy to hot-wire the engine. Whoever took it knew what they were doing."

"Or they had a key," Wade said.

His dad gave him a sage nod. "You think Brett Fortier arranged the theft himself?"

"Like you said, I wouldn't be here if his claim hadn't raised a red flag."

"Lot of things about that missing boat seem a little hinky," Sam said. "Why do you suppose he brought it up here from the Gulf? A craft like that would stick out like a sore thumb among the pontoon and ski boats. Plus, you don't need that kind of speed on a lake. You buy a boat like that if you're trying to impress someone. Or if you need to outrun another vessel on the open water."

"You might bring it up from the Gulf if you were trying to hide it from someone," Wade said. "Or conceal something onboard."

"Drugs? That wouldn't surprise me. Brett Fortier has always skated a little too close to the edge," Sam said. "I've heard rumors about him for years, about the kind of criminals he associates with. If even half of what they say is true, he could be mixed up in some nasty business. You need to watch your back with that one. You may not be the only one looking for his boat."

His dad's genuine concern made Wade regret even more the main reason for his visit. "This isn't my first rodeo. I know enough to be careful."

"See that you are. If you need help, you know where to find me."

"I'll be fine. Don't worry about me. Speaking of nasty business, there's another matter I came here to discuss with you. I went for a dive early this morning at the north end of the lake, where the old bridge went down. I didn't find Brett's boat, but I discovered a car on the bottom. Judging by the corrosion, I'd guess it's been down there for several years. I was wondering if you remember anything about a vehicle going over the bridge or if anyone filed a police report to that effect."

He watched his dad's face closely in the split second before he answered. He didn't flinch or glance away, but there was something indefinable in his eyes that might have been the flicker of a memory. Or Wade's imagination.

"Nothing was ever reported that I can recall offhand, but that spot was a hotbed of suspicious activity for years. Some of the guardrails were missing before the bridge was demolished. It would have been easy to roll a car off the side without anyone being the wiser."

"This isn't just any car," Wade said. "It's a Rolls Royce Wraith."

His dad had picked up his coffee cup, but now he set it back down with a clatter. "That's odd. You sure about that?"

Wade nodded.

Sam looked skeptical. "Water does a real number on metal. You're saying the vehicle is still in good enough shape that you could identify the make and model?"

"I recognized the body style, and the hood ornament is unmistakable," Wade said. "And I'd say *odd* is an understatement. Think about the implication. There's a Rolls Royce Wraith at the bottom of Shutter Lake. What's the probability that it's been down there ever since Eva Dallas McRae disappeared?"

His dad mopped at the spilled coffee with the same napkin he'd used to wipe ink from his fingers. "She didn't disappear, she left town."

"Never to be seen or heard from again," Wade reminded him.

Sam glanced up. "I'll admit the discovery is troubling, but nothing you've said so far convinces me the car is Eva's."

His denial reminded Wade of how hard Abby had initially resisted the truth. He presented his dad with the same rationale. "Have you ever known anyone else in the area to drive a car like that?"

"Could have been someone passing through town for all we know."

"That would be one hell of a coincidence," Wade said.

Sam's gaze narrowed as he studied Wade from across the table. "Where are you going with this?

You're pushing for answers like you've got a personal stake somehow. Does this have something to do with Abby Dallas being back in town?"

At the mention of her name, Wade felt a prickle of unease at the back of his neck. He hoped like hell she wasn't in any danger, but he had a bad feeling she just might be. "This isn't about Abby. It's about murder. Given your previous career, I would have thought you'd be a little more curious."

Sam's expression froze for a split second before he growled, "Murder? What the hell are you talking about?"

"Word's bound to get out, so I came here as soon as I could to give you a heads-up. I didn't just find a car at the bottom of the lake, Dad. Someone was inside when the vehicle went over the bridge. The skeletal remains of the victim are still handcuffed to the steering wheel."

A myriad of emotions flashed through Sam's eyes. He opened his mouth and then closed it again before glancing away. Finally, he said in strained voice, "You know this for certain?"

"Yes. I saw the remains through the window. Surprisingly, the cuffs are still intact. You would have thought the pressure would have pulled the wrist bone apart..." He trailed off with a grimace. "Anyway, the whole scene startled the hell out of me. I surfaced as soon as I found the remains and called the police. They've already sent divers down to verify. They'll have to bring the car up to make a positive identification, but the make and model of the car, along with the timing is suspect, to say the least."

Sam kept his gaze focused on the horizon. "I learned a long time ago not to jump to conclusions."

"We don't have to jump to conclusions. We'll know for a fact soon enough."

"The police are already on the scene, you say? Who's the lead?"

"A detective named Benson took my statement. Do you know him?"

He nodded. "Roy Benson. I know of him. He came onboard after I retired, but I hear good things. Smart, determined. A real hard-ass at times." Whatever emotion had been in Sam's voice a moment ago had given way to professional stoicism. "Maybe I should take a ride up there and see for myself what's going on."

"Why would you want to do that?" Wade said. "You're no longer on active duty."

"Why?" Sam shot him a frowning glance. "I was the police chief when we all thought Eva McRae skipped town with her lover. If it turns out she was murdered on my watch, then everything changes. I don't care how many years have

gone, it's still my responsibility to find out what happened. I owe it to her family."

"I thought you might feel that way," Wade said carefully. He couldn't tear his gaze from his dad's rigid profile. "You never suspected foul play back then?"

"There was no reason to. We had Eva's intentions and wishes in her own words. She planned to leave town and she didn't want to be followed."

"Still, a woman in her position goes missing, the thought must have crossed your mind that the situation might not be as it seemed."

He appeared irritated by Wade's persistence. "Easy to find fault with the benefit of hindsight. You're looking back through the lens of what you found this morning. All we knew at the time was that Eva left notes for her husband and her daughter. She put her affairs in order and made it clear she wasn't coming back anytime soon. In the eyes of the law, that was that."

"What about in your eyes?"

He sighed. "I made some inquiries, but maybe not enough if what you think is true. I talked to her family and business associates. I even had a chat with her attorney. To a person, they said she never appeared unduly stressed or under duress in the days leading up to her disappearance. She was very clear about her wishes and very precise with her instructions. By every indication, she was calm and in control."

"The amount of cash she withdrew didn't trigger an alarm?"

"Again, hindsight," his dad all but snapped. "Eva was a smart woman. She knew if she didn't want to be found or followed, she couldn't leave a digital trail while traveling. That meant no credit cards, no ATM withdrawals or bank transfers until she arrived at her destination."

Wade tried to keep his voice even, but a note of urgency slipped in as he leaned slightly forward. "Why do you think she was so insistent on not being followed? Did you ever wonder if she might have gotten mixed up in something dangerous or illegal? Is it possible she was being blackmailed? Maybe there was a reason she needed all that cash. Maybe she felt she had no choice but to disappear."

"I wondered about a lot of things," Sam said. "But a small-town police department operates on a limited budget. Sometimes you have to pick and choose where to allocate your manpower and resources. In Eva's case, I had to follow the evidence. As far as I or anyone knew, she left town of her own accord."

"What about the man she mentioned in Abby's note? Were there any rumors of an affair?"

"None that I ever heard."

"You never knew who she planned to meet the night she left town?"

His dad was silent for a moment. "I'm getting a

little tired of this third degree. I'll ask you again. Why is this so important to you?"

Wade cast a glance over his shoulder as he lowered his voice. "Because I'm afraid that man was you, Dad."

Chapter Four

Wade's father looked stunned, utterly aghast. His mouth went slack, and for a moment, he seemed incapable of speech. Then his hand shot across the table to grab Wade's wrist. His physical reaction startled Wade, and he jerked away reflexively.

His dad's eyes blazed with sudden anger. "What is wrong with you, bringing an accusation like that to my doorstep? Have you lost your mind? What if your mother heard you?"

Wade sent another uneasy glance toward the door. The last thing he wanted was to find his mother listening to their conversation through the screen. He kept his voice barely above a whisper as he met his dad's hard glare. "I haven't lost my mind. I only wish the explanation were that simple. I know about your affair. I saw the two of you together that summer. You and Eva."

His dad's mouth tightened. "You didn't see a damn thing. You need to stop this nonsense before you say something you can't take back. You have no idea what you're talking about."

Wade kept his own anger in check. "I know what I saw."

His dad stood abruptly, sending his chair flying backward. Without another word, he rounded the table and went down the steep stairs toward the dock. Wade waited a few minutes, then he rose, righted the chair and followed him down the steps. He didn't turn when Wade approached the dock. He stood with legs slightly apart at the edge of the platform staring down into the water. He seemed so intent that for a moment, Wade entertained the notion that he'd conjured Eva's ghost.

"I didn't come here with the intent to upset you," Wade said.

"You could have fooled me."

"I didn't come here to accuse you, either. I came because I thought you needed to know what I found."

"You came because deep down you're wondering if I had something to do with that car going over the bridge."

"I never said that."

His dad whirled. In the mottled light that sifted down through the trees, he appeared older than his fifty-nine years, rough-hewn and weary, but still with a hint of defiance in his eyes. "What is it you think you saw that summer?"

Wade hesitated, picking his way through a particularly awkward conversation. "I saw the two of you together at one of her rental houses one afternoon. I'd gotten off work early and took the boat out to test my overhauled motor. I guess I just happened to be in the right spot at the right time."

Sam looked livid. "That's it? You saw someone you thought was me from a distance?"

"It was you. I don't want to go into too much detail about what I saw, but…" A self-conscious silence followed. "Let's just say your body language was intimate. You had your arms around each other. You kissed. I assume the rental was where you'd meet that summer. That's why the house stayed vacant for so long. I drove by a few days later, and I saw your vehicle parked down the street."

Sam turned back to the water. "Was anyone with you?"

"No. I was alone both times."

"You never told anyone what you thought you saw?"

"No."

"What about Abby? Never a word even after her mother disappeared?"

"No, Dad. Not even then."

Sam was silent again.

Wade walked over to the edge of the dock, keeping space between them. Not because he was angry or disgusted—though a part of him still was—but because his dad had become a stranger to him once more. After he'd found out about Eva that summer, he'd come up with all sorts of excuses to stay away from home as much as possible. It wasn't just the guilt he felt for keeping a secret from his mother. Where he and his dad had once been close, he barely recognized the man across from him at the dinner table. He felt that same distance now.

"Did Mom know about the affair?"

"There was no affair," Sam insisted.

"I know what I saw, Dad."

"It was…" His shrug turned into a shudder. "I don't know what the hell it was. It wasn't love—I know that much. We met a few times and then it was over."

At least he was no longer denying the relationship, but a part of Wade wished that he would. Even though he'd lived with the secret of his father's betrayal for a long time, confirmation was still a hard blow. "How did it start?"

Sam scrubbed his face as if he could wipe clean his memories. "Is this really necessary? It was a long time ago."

"Given what I found at the bottom of the lake? Yeah, Dad. I think it's necessary."

"If it turns out to be her car…" He closed his eyes briefly. "I didn't know. If you believe nothing else, believe that. I didn't know."

Are you trying to convince me or Eva?

"Let's just take it one step at a time," Wade said. "Tell me how it started."

The contempt in his dad's voice was palpable. "The way those things usually start. With a weak man and a lonely woman."

Lonely? Eva? "She was unhappy in her marriage?"

"She and James McRae were never a good match. That's what she told me, at least. I think what she really meant was that he was no match for her. Eva could be a difficult woman. Reckless in her personal life and utterly ruthless in her business affairs."

"What about you and Mom?"

"I loved your mother then and I love her now. That will never change."

And yet...

Sam made a helpless gesture with his hand. "This isn't an excuse, but that summer was an especially rough time for her. There were days when she couldn't drag herself out of bed. I was under a lot of pressure at work and... Eva was Eva."

Sounded like an excuse to Wade.

He knew things happened in a marriage that only the two people involved could understand, but his instinct was still to come to his mother's defense. He forced himself to hold back. Until he knew the full story, he would do his best to reserve judgment. After all, he was far from perfect. He'd made mistakes. He knew only too well that things were not always the way they seemed. If he'd come clean with Abby, each of their lives might have been changed. Instead, he'd let her believe the worst about him because at the time, it had seemed the easiest way out for everyone.

"I get it, Dad. Eva was a beautiful woman and you're human."

Sam frowned. "Don't patronize me."

"I'm trying to keep an open mind," Wade said. "This isn't an easy conversation for a son to have with his father."

"We can stop right now, then. No need to go any further. You got what you came for."

"Not really. I'm still trying to make sense of it all," Wade said. "Tell me about Eva."

His dad sighed. "You don't ask for much, do you?"

"I'm trying really hard to understand. What was she like? What was she like to you?"

Sam gazed out over the lake, his eyes narrowing as he searched the distant shoreline. "She was like moonlight. Luminous. Seductive. But she had a dark side. I guess it was part of her allure. When she had you under her spell, she was like a drug. That's the best way I know to describe her effect on me. The high when we were together was like nothing I'd ever experienced before. She made you want things…need things—"

Wade put up a hand. "Okay, I get the picture."

"You wanted to know."

He only thought he had. "So how did it end?"

Sam drew a long breath and released it. "One morning I woke up stone cold sober and thought, 'What the hell am I doing?' The whole thing seemed like a bad dream. Like it happened to someone else. To this day, I can't reconcile being so foolish. I risked everything, and for what?" He shook his head as if he was still trying to puzzle it out.

"Was she upset when you broke things off?"

"Upset? She laughed and told me to lighten up. It was never meant to last."

"That must have stung."

"Not really. It was typical Eva. I was relieved, actually."

Wade wondered if that was true. Pride was a fragile thing. "You never saw her again?"

"I glimpsed her around town occasionally, but we never spoke."

"And you never told Mom," Wade said. "You didn't think she had a right to know?" Bitterness soured his tone despite his best efforts to remain neutral.

His dad's voice hardened. "I didn't think I had the right to cut her to the quick just to clear my conscience. You don't have that right, either."

"If I was going to tell her, don't you think I would have done so by now?" Wade took a moment to tamp down a burst of anger. He had to remind himself he hadn't come here to judge or condemn. He just wanted the truth. "I don't want to hurt her, either," he said in a hushed tone. "But it hasn't been easy keeping that secret from her. *Your* secret. For those first few months, every time I looked at her...every time I looked at *you*..."

His dad's stare said everything.

Wade ran a hand through his hair as he thought about what still needed to be said between them. He felt tired and guilty and disillusioned, and he just wanted to get in his boat and speed away. "I won't say anything, but she's bound to find out sooner or later. Secrets always have a way of coming out, even ten years after the fact."

"Just leave it alone." His dad's anger had vanished, and now he sounded numb.

"I wish I could, but I can't. I'm not the only one who'll have these questions. Have you even thought about that? This is a homicide investigation now. Once the police start actively pursuing leads, it's entirely possible someone else who knew about you and Eva will come out of the woodwork. Then the cops will wonder why you didn't come forward with the information at the time of her disappearance. They'll wonder why you didn't pursue your own leads. Look at it from an impartial point of view. Maybe you and Eva planned to leave town together, but you got cold feet at the last minute. Maybe she flew into a rage and threatened to tell Mom. One thing led to another…things got out of hand…" He didn't finish the thought.

"No one will believe that because it's not what happened," Sam said in that same emotionless voice.

"The police will ask questions, anyway. You don't think it would be better to get out ahead of this thing?"

His dad sighed. "What exactly are you suggesting?"

"Go to the police and tell them about the affair," Wade said. "You may be retired, but you're still one of them. You've earned their respect and the benefit of the doubt. They'll be discreet. It's the only way to keep it contained."

But his dad wasn't listening. He stood with that same rigid posture as his gaze traveled up the steps to the house. Wade turned to find his mother on the deck staring down at them.

WADE WAVED AND she lifted a hand in response. The effort seemed almost reluctant, though Wade told himself her hesitancy was only his imagination. They were far enough away that he didn't think she could have overheard their conversation, but voices did tend to carry on a breeze. There had been a few angry moments when they may not have been as careful as they should have been.

His father muttered something under his breath.

"How long do you think she's been standing there?" Wade asked.

"She wasn't there a minute ago when I checked. Anyway, she couldn't have heard us from this distance."

"I hope not."

But even if they were out of earshot, Laura Easton was a very perceptive woman. She'd know something was wrong from their expressions and body language. Wade made an effort to shake off the lingering bad taste from the unpleasant discussion as they started up the stairs. He took the lead and his dad followed a step behind him. He tried to gauge his mother's mood as he neared the top, but as sensitive as she was to his emotions, she'd always been difficult for him to read. He wondered if she'd learned to school her expression in order to hide the darkness that seemed to hover at arms' length even during the good times.

She wore a sleeveless yellow dress with a full skirt that fluttered in the breeze. From a distance, she looked like a young woman: tall, trim and tan. But like Sam, a closer inspection revealed lines in her face and shadows beneath her eyes. She waited until Wade stepped onto the deck, and then she came over and gave him a big hug. The tightness of her embrace was reassuring, and Wade returned it wholeheartedly.

"I'm so happy to see you." She reached up and touched his cheek. "Why did no one tell me you were coming?"

"It was spur of the moment," he said. "I needed to talk to Dad about a case I'm working on." That much was true. Still, he shot his dad an accusing glance for no other reason than it made him feel momentarily better.

She searched his face. "You look tired."

"Thanks, Mom."

"It wasn't an insult. A mother notices these things. You haven't been taking care of yourself."

"I didn't get much sleep last night, but I'm fine." He gently disengaged from the embrace. "I don't want to talk about me. Look at you, all dolled up. Is that a new dress?"

"This old thing? I've had it forever." She smoothed her hands down the skirt. "The style is a little young for me, but I drag it out now and then because the color makes me feel like I'm wearing sunshine."

Sunshine was the perfect foil for moonlight, Wade decided. "Looks good on you."

His deflection didn't quell her fretting. "If I'd known you were coming, I could have planned something special for lunch. As it is, there's not much in the house—"

"I wouldn't expect you to cook for me, and anyway, I can't stay. I've got a full day ahead of me."

"The boy is in town working a case," Sam reminded her. He stood with his back against a post, arms folded, his gaze meeting Wade's without darting away in guilt.

"But you have to eat," his mom protested.

"Another day, I promise."

She looked crestfallen. "Can you at least spare a few minutes to have coffee with your mother?"

How was he supposed to turn that down? "Just a quick cup, and then I really do have to go." Wade didn't know whether this was better or worse than he'd expected. His dad acted as though nothing had gone down between them, and his mom seemed perfectly fine. So why did he feel like the lowest of the low? Why did he feel as if he were the one who'd done something wrong?

His dad was still eyeing him. "I'll put on a fresh pot. Give you two a chance to catch up."

Instead of settling down at the table, his mother went over to the edge of the deck and stood gazing out at the scenery as people who lived on the water seemed to have a tendency to do. Wade understood. Why waste the view even for a moment?

"It's nice back here," he said. "Quiet. You don't hear all the Jet Skis like you do out on the lake."

"You don't have the expansive views, either, but I like the canal," she said dreamily. "The colors of the water are constantly shifting, and the light is so moody and reflective with all the trees.

When your dad first suggested we sell our house and buy this property, I was hesitant. I thought I would be lonely back here. I was so used to having everything I needed in town. But now I love it. I can't imagine living anywhere else."

"That's good. I'm glad you're happy here. Dad said you'd started painting again. I'd like to see some of your work."

"Maybe next time," she demurred. "I'm a bit rusty."

"No pressure," Wade said. "Whenever you're ready."

She gave him a sidelong glance. "Earlier when you were down on the dock with your dad, I couldn't help noticing the tension. I haven't seen either of you like that in a very long time. It made me remember how headstrong you both can be." She turned worriedly. "Is everything okay between you two?"

"Everything is fine, Mom."

"But you don't seem fine. I know you well enough to recognize when something is wrong. You look—"

"Tired?" He smiled.

"Anxious. Distracted. What's going on, Wade?"

He took a moment to answer. "The case I'm working on is complicated. It involves someone I used to know. Someone I didn't like. I don't want to let my personal feelings get in the way of my investigation."

"Who is this person?"

"Brett Fortier. His boat was stolen from the marina a couple of weeks ago. The insurance company hired me to make sure the claim he filed is legit."

"I see. Well, if you're talking about the same Brett Fortier from high school, then you're almost guaranteed to find something shady," she said. "He was always a pill."

Wade smiled at her mild description. "You used to say the same thing about me. I know I caused you and Dad more than a few gray hairs before I decided to grow up."

"Minor indiscretions compared to what you hear about these days." She reached over and gave his arm a squeeze. "Besides, you always had a good head on your shoulders and a kind heart. I never worried too much about you back then."

"But you do now?"

She sighed. "I think your work is a lot more dangerous than either you or your dad let on."

"It's really not. People do reckless things for an insurance settlement, and they sometimes do more reckless things to try and cover up their lies. There's an occasional hitch, but never anything I can't handle. Don't forget, I learned from the best."

"I hope that's true. Your dad was a good cop for a lot of years. His badge was so much a part of the man he became. He took great pride in serving his community, and he had a lot more years to give. Early retirement was his idea, but I know he left the department for me. I don't take that sacrifice lightly, so I want to thank you."

Wade was taken aback. "Me? Why?"

"I know it makes him happy that you still come to him for help."

Wade swallowed, wishing the relationship with his dad was still that simple. "Why wouldn't I want his help? Retirement hasn't dulled his instincts."

Her smile turned wry. "Yes, well, retirement hasn't turned out to be what either of us expected. His consulting business is starting to take up more and more of his time. The department has him working through a stack of cold cases. Did he tell you?"

"No, but I can understand why they'd want him. He always had an eye for detail. Now he can afford to take as much time as he needs to go through each file without having to split his attention between active cases." Wade paused, taking in his mother's furrowed brow. "You okay with this arrangement?"

"Yes, if it makes him happy. It's just..." Her eyes were shadowed when she turned. "Sometimes I think digging into those old cases does nothing but stir up a bunch of bad memories for people who've already suffered enough."

"Everyone deserves justice," Wade said.

"Even if the truth does more harm than good?"

"Even then."

"I wonder. Maybe some things really are best left in the past." She shrugged, but something dark flickered in the depths of her eyes, something that sent an inexplicable tingle across Wade's scalp. "Maybe some secrets are best left buried."

Chapter Five

After Wade left the cottage that morning, Abby cleaned up the terrace and then sat on the steps for the longest time, deep in thought. She needed to get on the road. A good four-hour drive lay ahead of her, and yet she lingered because she dreaded the conversation with her grandmother. And because she hadn't fully absorbed the news for herself. That was normal, she supposed. No matter how many years had gone by, the death of a loved one was hard to accept, but a cold-blooded murder was nearly impossible to process. So many conflicting emotions warred inside her. Disbelief, guilt, fear. Anger. She supposed that, too, was normal.

Below her, the cove remained quiet, but the buzz of activity out on the lake drifted up through the oleanders like the distant call of an old memory. Far from an intrusion, the noise of engines and laughter made her feel more connected and less alone. Less afraid.

She couldn't stop thinking about Wade's apprehension that she, too, could be in danger. In the space of a single morning, her whole world had changed. She told herself she should be relieved that at last she finally had an answer to her mother's disappearance, but deep down, she wished she could blink her eyes and make everything normal again. Her mother had died at the bottom of the lake, the secret of her demise hidden beneath murky waters for ten long years. There was no relief in that knowledge. No closure or acceptance, only more questions.

Abby had lived most of her adulthood in the shadow of her mother's abandonment. The seemingly callous desertion had colored every aspect of her life and relationships. She'd become guarded and timid, reluctant to trust. How could she not be? After so many years of protecting herself, what was she to do now with this new information, this profound revelation? Her mother hadn't left town of her own accord. She'd been handcuffed to the steering wheel of her beloved car before it had been pushed over the edge of the bridge.

The image of a woman struggling against time and rising water was a vision too terrible to contemplate, and yet Abby couldn't get the disturbing scene out of her head. She could almost feel the abject terror as the cold lake water closed in on her, the utter shock of betrayal and the panic of being trapped. That her mother's nightmare would have ended quickly did nothing to alleviate the horror of what had been done to her, possibly by someone she knew and trusted, someone she may even have loved.

But if one drilled down deep enough, certain facts remained the same. Her mother had likely meant every word she'd written in the note she'd left on Abby's dresser. She'd wanted to start a new life far away from her home and family, far away from her daughter, and she'd justified her action by reminding Abby that she'd be leaving for college soon. As if her age made everything all right. As if her coming adulthood meant Abby would no longer need a relationship with her mother.

A relationship she would never have now. Whatever faint hope she'd harbored in the deepest part of her heart for a mother-daughter reunion had been dashed by the cold, harsh reality of Wade Easton's discovery.

Wade Easton. She drew a long breath and released it. She couldn't afford to get distracted by dwelling on an old boyfriend. Time enough later to dissect and brood about *their* reunion. Time enough later to remind herself of *his* betrayal. At the moment, she needed to stay focused on the more immediate task at hand, namely, finding her mother's killer. Before she could even contemplate the seemingly impossible mission of solving a ten-year-old murder, she first had to break the news to her grandmother. The knowledge that her only daughter had been murdered would devastate the poor woman, which was why Abby had sat on the terrace steps procrastinating all morning. But it had to be done, sooner rather than later.

Hardening her resolve, she finally got up and went inside to pack an overnight bag before locking up the cottage. The long drive to Atlanta gave her plenty of time to worry and reflect. So much so that by the time she hit Saturday afternoon traffic in the city, she'd already worked herself into quite a state. She stopped by the condo to check the mail and water the plants even though a neighbor had agreed to take care of those chores while she was away.

She found a dozen more ways to kill time until the late afternoon sunshine streaming in through her front windows reminded her that twilight would soon fall, and the news of Wade's discovery was best delivered in daylight.

Maybe the revelation would come as something of a relief to her grandmother after the initial shock. She was getting on in years. She deserved to know what happened. For far too long, she'd been stuck in a hellish limbo, clinging to the notion that her daughter had done a selfish, reckless deed because the alternative was even harder to accept. But ten years was a long time. A decade of dwindling hope took a toll.

Her grandmother lived in the Inman Park area of Atlanta, a historic district of grand old homes surrounded by wrought iron fences and meticulously clipped hedges. Abby parked in the circular drive at the front of the house rather than pulling around to the back as she normally did. She rang the bell and waited, a part of her hoping that no one was home. A few seconds later, Lillian glanced out one of the long sidelights before pulling back the door. She was immaculately turned out as she always was in wide-leg linen trousers and a matching cream tunic intricately embroidered in shades of her signature blue at the neckline and sleeves. She'd pulled her silvery gold hair back into a sleek French twist, and her fingers and lobes were bejeweled in diamonds, platinum and her favorite sapphire ring.

"Abigail?" Her hand fluttered to her heart as she glanced over Abby's shoulder to the veranda as if checking to see if her granddaughter had come alone.

"Hi, Grandmother. Did I catch you at a bad time? You look as if you were on your way out."

"I had friends over earlier, but I'm alone now. This is a lovely surprise. I thought you'd already left for the lake." Her accent was pure Southern aristocracy, the drawled syllables softened by a slight tremor of age.

"I did leave, but I came back," Abby explained.

Her grandmother lifted a thin brow. "That was a quick trip. Did you change your mind?"

"No, I'm driving back tomorrow." She ran a nervous hand down the side of her jeans. "I'm sorry for just showing up without calling first. Do you have a minute? Can we talk?"

"You never need to call. You know that. This is still your home. But you're certainly being mysterious." Her grandmother moved aside so that Abby could step into the foyer.

"I don't mean to be." She leaned in and bussed the older woman's cheek, catching a whiff of her perfume before she drew away to close the door. The scent was fresh yet timeless, like a drop of vanilla splashed on crisp laundry. Abby drank in the comforting fragrance as her senses wallowed in the familiar appointments of vintage rugs, polished mahogany and sparkling chandeliers. "I'll tell you everything. It's just…maybe we should sit down first."

Diamonds flashed as her grandmother's hand once again crept to her throat. "Now you're starting to frighten me. Are you ill?"

"No, I'm perfectly fine as you can see. There's no reason to be afraid. Let's just sit."

Her grandmother led her down the long hallway to the informal den at the back of the house. Informal by her standards, anyway. She motioned Abby to a well-worn leather chesterfield sofa while she took a seat on a mohair armchair.

Perched on the edge, she remained silent and stoic as she waited for Abby to explain the reason for the impromptu visit.

The French doors were open, and Abby could smell jasmine from the garden. The scent conjured gauzy images of floral dresses and afternoon soirees from a forgotten era. She closed her eyes and drew in the bouquet of those romantic visions before she began to reveal to her grandmother the hard, ugly truth of her mother's demise. She started reluctantly and built momentum until everything came pouring out. Her grandmother sat quietly through it all, posture rigid, hands folded in her lap. But her blue eyes glittered as brilliantly as her diamonds as the news began to sink in.

Abby finished with a helpless shrug. "That's it. That's all I know at the moment. I'm so sorry to break it to you before we have a positive identification, but I didn't want you to hear the news from someone else."

Her grandmother got up and went over to the French doors, her back to Abby as she gathered her thoughts and poise. Neither of them spoke. Abby remained seated, giving her grandmother however much time and space she needed to digest the news.

"We can't make any arrangements until we know for certain," her grandmother finally said.

The practicality of the statement was a bit jarring to Abby. "No, I suppose not."

Her grandmother spoke softly, the drawl even more pronounced, but now there was steel around the edges. "Is it possible you could be mistaken?"

Abby cleared her throat and slid her splayed fingers over the tops of her thighs for lack of anything better to do with her hands. "As I said, we won't know conclusively until the medical examiner has a chance to compare dental and medical records. He may even need to run a DNA analysis. These things take time. But the make and model of the car, along with the location and timing…" She drew a breath. "There's also the fact that we haven't seen or heard from Mother in over a decade. I have to believe if she was still out there…still alive…one of the private detectives you hired would have found her by now."

"Not if she doesn't want to be found. Eva is a very resourceful woman."

But why wouldn't she want to be found?

"Either way, we'll know soon enough." Abby gentled her tone. "You should try to prepare yourself for the results."

"I suppose a part of me has been preparing for the past decade," her grandmother said in a resolved tone. "Still, it comes as a blow, doesn't it?" She placed her hand on the door frame for support. Abby wanted to go to her, but she didn't. Lillian Jamison was a very proud, very strong woman. She would come to Abby when she was ready.

"You say the Easton boy found the car?"

"Wade Easton, yes." Abby's heart thumped at the mention of his name. The sound of it came as another jolt in the quiet of her grandmother's den. "He's an investigator these days. People hire him to find lost things. He was looking for a stolen boat when he came upon the car."

"I remember him." Her grandmother remained at the open doorway, staring out into the fading light as if she couldn't yet bring herself to turn and meet Abby's gaze. As if she wasn't quite ready to face the undeniable truth in her granddaughter's eyes. "I met him once when I came to Fairhope for a visit. Very polite young man. Good-looking, like his father, but trouble."

Abby said in surprise, "You knew his dad?"

"Only in passing. Your grandfather and I kept our house on the lake for years after we moved to Atlanta. He made a point of getting to know the local authorities so they would keep an eye on the place while we were away."

"Did you know Sam Easton became the police chief? I understand he's retired now," Abby said.

"Retired?" Lillian's voice turned wistful. "I remember him as a young officer. Time does fly, doesn't it?"

Abby hesitated, not quite sure what to do or say next. She cleared her throat again and smoothed another imaginary crease from her jeans. "I suppose Wade Easton is one of the few things on which you and Mother were in agreement. She didn't approve of our relationship. She thought he'd hold me back, whatever that meant. I never really understood why she disliked him so much."

Her grandmother turned at that. "She saw the way he looked at you. And the way you looked at him. As much as Eva seemed to thrive in Fairhope, she wanted something more for you. As did I. And just look at you now. All grown up. Poised, confident. Successful in your own right. Eva would be so proud. I certainly am."

Abby wasn't so sure about any of that. Most days she felt like an imposter, as if she'd left the real Abigail Dallas behind when she'd fled to Atlanta ten years ago. She wasn't a born entrepreneur like her mother. She wasn't savvy or gutsy or intuitive. She didn't like taking risks. Yes, she'd carved out a successful career for herself in commercial real estate, but sometimes she wondered if it was even what she wanted. Maybe a part of her had still been trying to please and impress her mother. Maybe she felt the need to prove herself before she went back to Fairhope and took the reins of Eva's business.

Her grandmother closed the French doors against the falling twilight and came back over to sit beside Abby on the sofa. She looked composed and determined as she took her granddaughter's hand. "I needed a moment to wallow, but that's over now. I want to focus on you. You've been remarkably calm and steadfast. I can't imagine how difficult it was for you to even come here. None of this has been easy for either of us."

"To be honest, I think I'm still in shock, too," Abby said. "We spent so many years wondering and searching and hoping—"

"And all that time, she was at the bottom of Shutter Lake."

The bluntness startled Abby. "Yes."

Her grandmother squeezed her fingers. "I always wanted to believe she was out there in the world, happy and healthy despite the misery and turmoil she left behind. I didn't want to accept the possibility that she might actually be dead. Not without proof. But it never really made sense that she wouldn't eventually get in touch with us. That she could so easily leave her business and her only child behind forever." Her mouth tightened as her voice hardened. "God knows, Eva could be callous and selfish, and if I'm brutally honest, she was never cut out to be a wife and mother. But she did love you in her own way. She was very proud of the young woman you were becoming."

"Grandmother…" Abby clasped her hand in both of hers. "Who do you think could have done something like that to her?"

"I don't know, child."

"Do you know of any enemies she had? Someone with a grudge who'd want to hurt her?"

She lifted a thin shoulder. "Eva could be single-minded, even cruel, when she went after something she wanted, whether in her personal life or business. I'm certain there were any number of people with axes to grind. I don't pretend to understand what drives a person to murder, but I suppose one would have to start with the most obvious suspect."

"You mean James."

She nodded. "I always believed him to be a good man. Forgiving to a fault and in some ways, far too sensitive for Eva. She needed someone who could give back as good as she gave, and James wasn't that man. He was too besotted. Too much of a pleaser. She had that effect."

"What about my dad? Were he and my mother a good match? I'm sorry to say, I don't even remember what he looked like, let alone how he and Mother interacted."

Lillian patted her arm absently. "They were so young when they married. Still in that first blush of love when he was killed. It's impossible to know if they would have lasted. All I can say for certain is that they were very much in love at the time."

"She had no other serious relationships until James? She was still a young woman. Fifteen years is a long time to be alone."

"She certainly had her chances. Eva never lacked for admirers, but she was too busy building her empire to settle down. She didn't take any of the suitors seriously, but she loved the attention."

"Then how did she end up with James, if they were so ill-suited?"

"I've asked myself that very question," she admitted. "My only answer is that for your mother, the grass was always greener."

Abby thought about that for a moment. "I keep going back to what she said in the note. She'd fallen deeply in love. The kind of love that happens once in a lifetime. If her feelings for this man were so strong and so consuming that she was willing to leave her family and business for him, how did she manage to keep the relationship secret? Someone must have seen them together. Surely over time she would have let something slip to James. Did you know that she was seeing someone behind his back?"

"No, but it didn't surprise me," her grandmother said. "After all, James was married when they first met. He left his first wife for Eva. Although according to her, the marriage was already over. She just provided an easy way out for both of them."

Abby winced at her mother's justification for breaking up a marriage. It seemed she could rationalize almost anything so long as she ended up with what she wanted. "That divorce goes a long way in explaining Lydia's attitude," Abby said. "She could be rude, even savage at times. I often wondered why she left her mother to come live with us when she seemed to resent everything about her father's new marriage."

Her grandmother made a look of disdain. "One could sympathize if she hadn't been such a wretched young woman."

"Maybe she had reason to be."

Her grandmother bristled at the suggestion. "No one has a right to be that unpleasant. I really don't think James would have hurt Eva, no matter what he found out about her. He was that much in love with her. But I can't say the same for his daughter. You asked why Lydia left her mother. Maybe she had no choice. Maybe her mother was as exhausted and disgusted by her attitude as the rest of us."

"Grandmother." The rebuke was only half-hearted.

Her chin lifted. "It's true and you know it. A very odd duck, that one. If you ask me, she was far too involved in her father's personal life. Protective and possessive to an unhealthy degree. And such deplorable manners." She tsk-tsked with an exaggerated shudder. "You're right about her feelings for Eva. She made no bones about how deeply she despised my daughter."

"Resented, yes, but *despised* might be a bit strong," Abby said.

"Not strong enough if some of the things Eva claimed were true. I don't know why she put up with her. I would have sent her packing, but Eva thrived on chaos. I sometimes think she egged it on."

"Lydia didn't need much encouragement," Abby murmured.

"She had a huge chip on her shoulder," her grandmother agreed. "But despite all that, I notice she's had no problem living in Eva's house all these years, and she's burrowed herself like a tick in the business. When you think about it, she's basically taken over Eva's life. Now doesn't that just make you wonder?"

Abby had started to wonder about a lot of things since Wade's visit to her that morning. So many questions churned in her head. A part of her wanted to crawl in bed and pull the covers over her head while another side wanted to drive back to Shutter Lake that very night so that she could start digging for the truth.

"You don't seriously think Lydia would have hurt Mother, do you?"

"Someone did."

"I know but—"

"People do all sorts of despicable things for all kinds of reasons," Lillian insisted. "I'm telling you, there was something seriously wrong with that woman. The more I think about it, the more convinced I am that she was somehow involved in Eva's death."

Abby glanced at her grandmother in alarm. Her jaw was rigid, her cheeks bright pink with anger. "We don't know anything yet. It's best not to jump to conclusions. In fact, maybe we shouldn't talk about this anymore. You're upset, and the last thing I want to do is make things harder for you."

"I disagree. I think it's important that we get everything out in the open. We both have questions. We both want to know what happened. It's normal to speculate. How can we not, knowing what we now know?"

"As long as the speculation doesn't leave this room," Abby cautioned.

"Oh, don't worry. I'm not about to confront Lydia McRae, no matter how much I'd like to shake the truth out of her. I'll leave her to the police if that's where the evidence takes them. This conversation is just for you and me."

Abby nodded. "That's the way it has to stay for now. At the very least, we need to give the police time to make the notifications."

Her grandmother gave her a sidelong look. "And yet here you are telling me everything. Am I supposed to feign ignorance when they call?"

"I trust you'll know how to handle the situation," Abby said. "But as long as we're playing armchair detectives…"

She leaned forward, seemingly keen to continue. "Yes, go on."

Abby hesitated. "Are you sure you want to talk about this? I don't want to upset you any more than I already have."

"Of course, I'm sure," she said in an irritated tone. "I know you mean well, Abigail, but I'm not some fragile old woman you need to protect. My mind is as sharp as ever. Besides, talking things through is far better than brooding alone in my room for the rest of the evening."

"For me, too," Abby agreed. "The thing I keep coming back to is the money. Why do you suppose she withdrew all that cash before she left? She'd already transferred enough funds into her private accounts to live on indefinitely. Why did she need the cash? Blackmail? Bribery? Was she in some kind of trouble? I find myself coming up with all these disturbing scenarios. I can't help wondering if she had a lover at all. Maybe she needed to disappear and concocted a story that she knew would keep us from coming after her."

"Anything's possible, I suppose." Her grandmother fingered the intricate embroidery at her neckline. "Other than her clashes with Lydia, she never said anything to me about trouble at work or in her personal life, but then she wouldn't. I was never her confidante. Not about serious matters."

"I don't think anyone was. For as long as I can remember, Mother was secretive and distant. In some ways cold. She kept things close to her chest."

"All by design," her grandmother fretted. "From a very early age, she purposely cultivated an air of mystery. She never wanted anyone to know the real Eva. Not even me."

"Or me. But I do know one thing. Neither of us will have any peace until we find out who killed her."

Her grandmother's voice sharpened. "I don't like the sound of that, Abigail. Remember what you told me about keeping the speculation to ourselves. You need to heed your own advice. I don't want you getting involved in anything dangerous. Let the police do their job while you keep a safe distance. The more I think about it, the more prudent I believe it would be for you to stay here with me until everything is resolved. I couldn't bear it if anything were to happen to you. Promise me you won't do anything rash."

Abby mustered a wry smile. "Grandmother, when have you ever known me to do anything rash? I always think through everything to death before I act. Please don't worry. I won't do anything risky or foolish, but someone needs to be there to keep the police on their toes. A case this old has a tendency to get pushed to the wayside. I won't let that happen."

Lillian sighed. "I know that look. You've already made up your mind."

"I have to go back. It's not just a matter of keeping the police honest. Someone needs to be there when…" *They bring her up.* Abby suppressed a shiver at the image. "In case they need a DNA sample."

"I can see we're not going to agree on this, but I'll let the matter rest for the night. We can talk more in the morning. Sunshine always brings a clearer perspective."

Not about murder, Abby thought.

FOR THE REST of the evening, they talked about other things—Abby's job, her grandmother's charity work, the garden club, how downtown traffic had become an absolute nightmare. Mindless topics to take their minds off what lay beneath Shutter Lake. When they got hungry, Abby ordered dinner and her grandmother opened a bottle of wine. They sat at the big dining room table and ate takeout by candlelight. Afterward, her grandmother went off for a soak in the tub while Abby cleared the table and locked up.

When she finally crawled into bed and dozed off, she had the strangest nightmare. She could see herself swimming underwater among tall steel girders and mountains of broken concrete only to discover her mother sitting on the hood of her Rolls Royce, smiling in that enigmatic way she had as she beckoned Abby to join her. But Abby couldn't move. All of a sudden, she found herself trapped inside the car and running out of air as she pounded on the window, desperate to get her mother's attention.

She woke up gasping for breath and clutching the covers, her frantic gaze darting about in the dark for a landmark. Then everything came back to her. She was in her old bedroom in her grandmother's house in Atlanta. She'd come here to tell her about Wade's discovery.

The familiarity of her surroundings did little to calm her racing heart. Panic had set in, and she couldn't seem to talk herself down. For the first time since Wade had shown up at the cottage, she felt truly afraid. Not just an uneasy prickle, but the kind of paralyzing terror that made her want to cower under the covers until daylight.

Someone had murdered her mother in a cruel and deliberate way. The method and timing took planning. No crime of passion, no momentary loss of control. Eva had been lured out to the old bridge and caught unaware by someone she knew and trusted. Someone for whom she had no fear.

Maybe Wade was right. Maybe Abby's inheritance had already made her a target, too.

The longer she lay in the dark with that creeping fear, the more convinced she became that something was amiss in the house.

As quietly as she could, she threw off the covers and swung her legs over the side of the bed, sitting on the edge for a moment as she searched every shadowy corner of that moonlit room. The balcony doors were closed to the night. She'd double-checked the lock before getting into bed, but she'd left the curtains open so that she didn't feel quite so claustrophobic.

Unlocking the doors, she stepped onto the balcony, her gaze lifting to the night sky before dropping to the garden below. The night was warm and balmy with only a mild breeze to stir the leaves. Nothing moved that she could detect. No barking dogs to alert the neighborhood of a prowler, no stealthy shadows slipping through the lush foliage. And yet she couldn't shake the feeling that something was very wrong.

She went back inside, locked the doors behind her and then padded across the thick rug to the hallway door. Poking her head out, she glanced both ways before leaving the safety of her room. Moonlight streamed in through the large window over the stairwell. She could see her way well enough without turning on any lights, which was good. She didn't want to alarm or disturb her grandmother in the middle of the night.

Easing down the curving stairway, she winced as the risers creaked beneath her bare feet. She cut through the foyer to the hallway, bypassing the formal living and dining rooms until she stood in the doorway of the den where she and her grandmother had sat earlier. The room lay in shadows except for a puddle of moonlight that streamed across the flagstone terrace and leeched through the French doors. A silhouette stood at those doors peering into the house.

Abby reacted instinctively. In the split second before the figure moved, she grabbed a poker from the fireplace hearth. Then she realized the person was on the inside looking out. "Grandmother? It's after midnight. What are you doing up?"

"Shush."

Abby lowered her voice. "What's wrong?"

"Someone's out there."

Her grandmother sounded strangely calm, almost detached. Abby's fingers tightened around the brass handle of the poker. "You saw someone in the garden just now?"

She said in a harsh whisper, "Don't turn on the lights!"

Abby kept the poker at her side as she hurried across the room to join her grandmother. She put her other hand on her grandmother's arm. "Are you okay? Should I call the police?"

She didn't turn or react to Abby's touch. Her gaze remained fixed on the garden. "Don't do anything. Just be still and watch."

Abby wanted to know who or what she was watching for, but she did as she was told, staring out into the darkness as her heart pounded and her hand around the metal handle grew clammy. In the dead of night, her elegant grandmother seemed somehow diminished, a frail and frightened old woman. Abby wanted to put a protective arm around her shoulders, but she was afraid to make a move, let alone to touch her again. What if she was sleepwalking? That would account for her strange behavior. Abby had always heard it could be dangerous to awaken a sleepwalker abruptly.

"Shush."

The sharp rebuke startled Abby. She hadn't said anything. She'd hardly dared to even breathe.

"Can you see her?" her grandmother whispered.

"I don't see anyone," Abby whispered back. "If someone's in the garden, shouldn't we call the police?"

"The police would only frighten her away. Just be quiet. She'll come back. I know she will."

"Who?"

"My Eva."

A chill shot down Abby's backbone. "Grandmother, she's not out there. She can't be. You know that, right?"

"But I saw her."

"You only thought you did. Don't you remember what we talked about earlier?" Abby chose her words carefully and kept her voice tender. "Someone found Mother's car at the bottom of Shutter Lake yesterday morning."

Her grandmother turned, eyes glittering in the moonlight. "The sapphire Wraith?"

"Yes."

"She loved that car."

"I know she did."

"She would never have left it behind."

Her family, yes, but not her car.

Abby grew even more uneasy. Had her grandmother blocked their previous conversation from her mind? Would she have to break the news to her all over again?

"Grandmother, what do you remember about the discussion we had before dinner?"

She sighed. "I remember every word of it. Don't worry, child. I haven't lost my mind. I know it can't really be Eva. Not after all these years." She swayed and Abby gripped her arm to steady her.

"It's okay, Grandmother. I'm here. Everything will be okay," she soothed, although they both knew nothing would be okay for a very long time.

"I had a dream about her before I woke up," her grandmother told her. "I suppose I became confused because she seemed so vivid to me. As if she were right there in the room with me."

"I dreamed about her, too, Grandmother."

"She called me Mommy the way she did when she was a little girl. I wanted so badly for that dream to be real."

"I know."

She drew a shuddering breath. "She was such a precocious child. She knew how to wrap me around her little finger even back then. I would forgive her anything, even when she misbehaved." Her voice cracked with emotion. "Do you think she was trying to tell me something?"

"I think it was just a dream," Abby said.

"She's really dead, isn't she? My Eva is gone."

"I think so. I'm sorry, Grandmother."

She turned back to the window, pulling her robe even more tightly around her as she shivered. "Then who is out there in my garden?"

Chapter Six

Abby edged closer to the door to probe the terrace and the darkness beyond as she reached a hand to check the dead bolt. The doors were locked. She'd made sure all the exits were secure and had activated the security system before going up to bed. No one could get inside without their knowing. As for the intruder in the garden, her grandmother had probably glimpsed a bush or a tree branch swaying in the breeze. She'd already been upset from the dream and was still half dazed with grief. Her imagination had played tricks on her in the moonlight. She'd seen what she wanted to see.

But even as Abby moved away from the French doors, the sound of shattering glass stopped her dead in her tracks. She was almost afraid to turn around, but then she realized the breach had come from the front of the house, not behind her. A second later, the overwhelming blare of the security alarm threatened to wake the dead.

She and her grandmother stood frozen until

Abby finally collected herself and said over the alarm, "Stay here and call 911."

"The security company will send the police."

"Call anyway, just to be certain."

Her grandmother grabbed her arm. "Where are you going?"

Abby clutched the poker. "Please, just make the call, Grandmother. And don't leave this room until I come back."

"Abigail, be careful."

The frightened missive followed her through the door and out into the hallway. Hugging the wall, she made her way past all the open rooms and into the foyer. Shards of glass lay glistening on the floor where one of the sidelights had shattered. She stepped gingerly through the sharp fragments to check the dead bolt. Still engaged, though she wouldn't have been surprised at that point to see an arm snake through the broken window to turn the lock. She waited, heart pounding, with her weapon at the ready. When no further assault was forthcoming, she entered the code to turn off the alarm and then turned to scan the foyer. Something rested on the floor just beneath the console table.

She bent and rolled the rock toward her with the end of the poker. A piece of paper had been folded into a neat square and taped to the side. A blunt way to get someone's attention, Abby thought. The delivery method almost seemed to be a statement, as if the brashness of the vandalism was a clue.

Abby knew better than to handle the evidence. Common sense told her to remain calm and wait for the police. *Don't do anything hasty.* The rock and the note would need to be dusted for prints, but she ignored her better instincts. She picked up the stone, testing the weight in her palm before carefully removing the paper. Inside the folds, someone had scrawled two words in angry red marker: STAY AWAY.

"What's that?"

She jumped at the sound of her grandmother's voice from the doorway. Slipping the note in the pocket of her robe, she turned with the rock still in her hand. "Someone threw this through the side window." When her grandmother started toward her, she cried, "Stop! Stay where you are, Grandmother. There's broken glass all over the floor. The pieces are sharp enough to cut right through your slippers."

"What about you?"

"I had to check the door to make sure it was still locked, but I'm trying to be careful."

Her grandmother pointed to the rock. "Should you have picked that up?"

"I...wasn't thinking clearly." She bent and placed the stone on the floor where she'd found it. "The police should still be able to pull prints if any were there to begin with."

"Abigail!"

She started guiltily. "Yes, Grandmother?"

"Why would someone throw a rock through my window? I've always felt perfectly safe here."

"No place is perfectly safe," Abby said.

Her grandmother hugged her arms around her body.

"Did you phone the police?"

"Yes."

Abby picked her way through the glass and put an arm around her grandmother's shoulders. "Go back to the den while I check the rest of the house. I want to make sure there's no other damage."

"Can't the police do that?"

"Yes, but it'll give me something to do while we wait. I won't be long, I promise."

When she'd seen her grandmother safely back to the den, Abby made the rounds through all the rooms. By the time she returned to the foyer, she barely had time to glance at the note a second time before a patrol car pulled to the curb, flashing blue lights reflecting ominously off the jagged fragments scattered across the floor.

She spent the next several minutes giving her statement to the two young officers who had responded to the 911 call. She didn't mention the note, let alone remove it from her pocket and hand it over to them. She wasn't sure why. At that point, she hadn't had a chance to think it through yet. She told herself she wanted to protect her grandmother. The shock of the broken window coming as it had on the heels of Abby's terrible news had shaken her to the core. It was one thing to believe her house had been randomly violated by malicious vandals, quite another to discover her sanctuary had been deliberately targeted, perhaps by her daughter's killer. She was already anxious about Abby's return to the lake. Why distress her further by revealing the note?

The rationalization came a little too easy. Maybe she was her mother's daughter after all, Abby thought. And now she took her justification a step farther. What would happen to the note if she turned it over to the police? They would log it into evidence and then toss it into a secure locker never to be seen again. Wouldn't it be more useful to take the note back to Fairhope and compare the scrawl to handwriting samples she could pull from the files at her mother's company? She didn't know much about handwriting analysis, but luckily, she knew an investigator who could probably point her in the right direction.

The notion of working alongside Wade Easton to solve her mother's murder was as disconcerting as it was stimulating. She had no wish to revisit an old romance, but like it or not, she and Wade had unfinished business. Even after all these years, the way their relationship had ended still stung. What better way to put those old feelings to rest once and for all than a daily reminder of his dishonesty?

She wasn't at all sure he would agree to such an arrangement, but he owed her. And if he resisted, well, she could be persuasive in her own right.

AFTER THE POLICE LEFT, Abby found a board in the basement and hammered up a makeshift barricade until she could call her grandmother's handyman first thing in the morning and have the glass replaced. Once again, she and Lillian said good-night, but Abby doubted either of them would get a wink of sleep after all the havoc. She tossed and turned as doubts and suspicions plagued her. Maybe her grandmother was right. Maybe she should stay in Atlanta until the police found her mother's killer.

But resolve returned with the sunrise. She saw to the window repair and even managed to persuade her grandmother to spend a few days in Savannah with her sister, Abby's great aunt. Abby purchased the ticket, drove her to the airport and arranged for a cousin to pick her grandmother up on the other end.

Satisfied that she'd done everything she could to keep her grandmother safe, she headed back to the lake, arriving in Fairhope at four in the afternoon. Instead of driving straight out to the cottage, she stopped by the house in town. The police had had plenty of time to alert her stepfather about her mother, but Wade seemed to think notifications might be delayed until the medical examiner could make a positive identification. Sooner or later, word would get out, but if James and Lydia remained in the dark, then this might be Abby's only opportunity to ask a few subtle questions before their guards went up.

She parked at the curb rather than pulling into the driveway so that she could sit for a moment and contemplate how to go about a covert interview. She worried that her expression or a slip of the tongue might give her away, but she had one thing going for her. If neither James nor Lydia knew about Eva, then they had no reason to suspect Abby's motives.

Again, the justification for her duplicity came a little too easy. Everything that had transpired since her arrival in Fairhope had led her to this point. She now knew her mother had been murdered. Handcuffed to the wheel of the car she'd loved so much before the vehicle had been pushed off the bridge. The scene unfolded in her head, and she found herself gripping the wheel of her own car as her mind drifted back to the final conversation with her mother. And even farther back to their last argument over her relationship with Wade.

I have nothing against the young man, but he's not the right sort for you.

Not the right sort? Do you have any idea how offensive that sounds?

You know what I mean. He's small-town. Conventional. From what I can tell, he lacks ambition.

We're small-town, Mother.

It's not the same thing and you know it. If you tie yourself to someone like Wade Easton, you'll never realize your full potential. In time you'll grow bored of him. You'll come to resent him for holding you back.

Is that the voice of experience?

Her mother had left the room without answering.

A few days later, Abby had awakened to find a note on her dresser with her name scrawled across the envelope in her mother's handwriting.

Abby shook off the memory as she became aware of a dark gray sedan facing toward her on the opposite side of the street. The vehicle was nondescript with no markers or adornments, and the windows were lightly tinted. Even so, she could have sworn the person behind the wheel was staring straight at her. A tingle of alarm shot through her. Was someone watching the house, or had she been followed all the way back from Atlanta?

She lifted her phone and snapped a photo of the car before she got out and crossed the street. Pausing on the sidewalk, she gave the sedan a hard scrutiny before she walked through the brick pillars on either side of the walkway. She could barely see the driver through the glare of sunlight on the windshield, but she made a mental note of her initial impression. Short hair, glasses, slender build. And he seemed to be watching the house or her or both.

Probably nothing. Just someone visiting next door.

Abby tried to put him out of her head as she started up the steps to the veranda, but too much had happened for her to completely dismiss a stranger. She glanced over her shoulder. He was still there. Still watching.

For a moment, she thought about going back out to the street and confronting him. Rap on the glass until he lowered his window and then demand that he state his name and business. She didn't, of course. Discretion was not only advised but also necessary.

She turned back to the house, the scent of jasmine nearly overpowering in the late-afternoon heat. Closing her eyes, she took a deep breath as memories once again assailed her. She and her mother had moved into this house when Abby was ten. It had been just the two of them until one weekend after her fifteenth birthday when her mother had come back from a business trip. She'd sat Abby down and told her that she and James McRae had eloped. He and his nineteen-year-old daughter, Lydia, would be living with them from now on.

James had moved in first, and Abby still remembered her first impression of him—a tall handsome man with vivid blue eyes and an easy smile. She'd liked him from the start. Her own dad had died when she was a baby, so she had no lingering feelings of resentment, no comparisons or a secret hope that her parents would someday get back together.

The few months that the three of them had lived together had been congenial and surprisingly fun. Abby had enjoyed James's quiet sense of humor. He was like a soothing balm to her mother's sometimes frenetic energy. When Lydia came, it was as if someone had thrown a live grenade into the house.

The day she moved in, she brought two suitcases and a boatload of drama and resentment. She didn't like her room or anything about the house, the street, the neighbors. She especially didn't like her new family and never wasted a chance to let Abby know just how galling she found the fifteen-year-old. Everyone had breathed a sigh of relief when she returned to college in the fall, though no one would admit it. The house once again became quiet and peaceful except on the occasional weekend when Lydia came for a visit. Abby could put up with her stepsister's surliness in small doses. She just learned to avoid her. Everything changed after Eva disappeared. Lydia transferred to a local school, moved back into the house and took charge. No one tried to stop her, least of all Abby. Maybe in time, she would have mustered enough gumption to push back, but once Wade was no longer in the picture, she found it easier to live with her grandmother and let Lydia have free rein over the house and later the business.

Hardening her resolve, Abby started up the steps. Her stepfather was seated on one of the cushioned chairs, eyes closed, head reclined against the back. She could see the hint of a five-o'clock shadow on his lower face, and his hair was a bit unkempt, but he was fully dressed in khakis and a white pullover shirt. Not the same dapper man from the early days, but that was understandable given the circumstances. Overall, he looked much better than Abby had expected.

He appeared to be sleeping, but his eyes flew open when a floorboard creaked beneath her feet.

Squinting into the sun behind her, he said hesitantly, "Abby?"

She winced. "I'm so sorry. I didn't realize you were napping until I'd already started up the steps."

He sat up straighter and motioned for her to join him. "I wasn't asleep. Just enjoying a little fresh air. It's actually quite pleasant underneath the ceiling fans. Come sit with me."

"I don't want to intrude. You need your rest."

"Nonsense. All I've been doing is resting. Please, sit with me. I'd love the company. I've been holed up in the hospital and now this house for far too long."

She tried to analyze his expression and tone as he shuffled aside a book on the round table next to his chair. He seemed calm and genuinely happy to see her. She could only take that to mean the police had yet to pay him a visit. He didn't know about Eva.

He smiled as she took a chair on the other side of the table. "I never got the chance to thank you for the lovely flowers you had sent to my room. I'm not much of a gardener, but I've always been partial to freesias."

"I know. You told me once your mother grew them outside your bedroom window when you were a boy."

His brows shot up. "You remember that?" He looked pleased.

"I'm sorry I didn't come see you in the hospital. I was told you weren't allowed visitors."

"Yes, they're very strict about that sort of thing these days. No matter. You're here now."

Keeping the secret of her mother's death was harder than she thought it would be. James had doted on Eva. By every indication, he'd been deeply in love with her. She didn't feel right withholding information of that magnitude. But then she reminded herself that the spouse was always a suspect. Maybe James had known all along her mother was dead, and he'd had ten long years to learn how to hide his guilt.

She tried to imagine him in a life-and-death struggle with her mother, watching stone-faced from the bridge as her car sank to the bottom of the lake.

"Abby? Are you okay?"

She jumped slightly at the sound of his voice and then looked around uneasily. "I was hoping to find Lydia at home. I wanted to talk to her about a couple of the reports she emailed to me."

He seemed to observe her as carefully as she studied him. "She's inside somewhere. Should I go look for her?"

"No, never mind. The questions can wait until tomorrow. Let's just have a nice visit." She settled back in her chair. "I must say, you're looking even better than I'd hoped."

"You're lucky you didn't see me a few days ago." His smile turned into a grimace. "I'm told I looked only slightly less dead than a corpse."

"You've had a rough time of it," she said. "But your color is coming back now, and you look rested. Lydia said the doctors are pleased with your progress."

"So they tell me. I should be back to work in a matter of weeks. In the meantime, I appreciate you coming down here to lend a hand. Lydia would never admit it, but she's overwhelmed. Summers are always busy, but this year has been especially chaotic, what with all the renovations we've undertaken. We put off what we could until the end of the busy season, but some things like plumbing and roof repairs just can't wait until fall. Your willingness to pitch in is a lifesaver."

"I'm happy to do whatever I can to ease the pressure."

He nodded. "You've always been a hard worker, and you've done well for yourself. That you'd take a leave from your own career to help us out means the world to me."

Well, it's still technically my mother's company. Why wouldn't I help? She merely nodded. "It's not a big deal. I have a lot of vacation time coming." She tucked back her hair and lifted her face to the breeze. "You're right. It's pleasant out here under the fans."

"How about a glass of lemonade? There's a pitcher in the kitchen, freshly squeezed. Hard to beat on a hot summer day."

He started to get up, but Abby said, "Sit tight. I'll get it. That is, if you don't mind me wandering around the house."

"It's your house, too," he said.

"In that case, two lemonades, coming up."

Abby got up and let herself in through the front door. She stood in the foyer for a moment, casting a curious gaze over the interior. Her first thought was that she might be able to find samples of handwriting that she could compare to the warning note. Her second impression was that the house had undergone a number of changes since she moved out ten years ago. She'd been back for a few brief visits but had never noticed until now just how extensive the transformation was. Different flooring, different paint, different furniture. Even the artwork had been swapped out, including a portrait of her that had once hung at the top of the stairs. Nothing of her mother's taste remained. Every trace had been relegated to a storage unit or the trash bin. Fair enough. She supposed it was only natural that James and Lydia would want to make the place their own.

For a moment, she was tempted to go up and have a look inside her old room. Not that she expected to find any of her mementos. Lydia had always coveted the front bedroom. She probably hadn't waited a full day after Abby left to move her stuff down the hallway.

Sunlight glistening off the edge of a gold frame drew her attention to a marble console table. She moved across the foyer and picked up the photograph. Apparently, not everything from the past had been banished. That a picture of her mother had been allowed to remain on display in such a prominent location shocked Abby. She stared down at her mother's face, remembering events and conversations that had taken place in the house, remembering the good times as well as the bad. Eva had been a complicated, secretive woman. Sometimes kind, rarely affectionate and always calculating.

"He won't allow me to put that one away," a voice said from the top of the stairs.

Abby glanced up as her stepsister came down a few steps and paused. She wore jeans, sandals and a simple cotton shirt, but even in her casual attire, she projected an air of formality and aloofness that seemed deliberately off-putting. Her dark hair was cut and styled in the same precision bob she'd worn for years, and her makeup was subtle and expertly applied. At thirty-three, she'd matured into a very attractive woman, but the hardness in her expression and a hint of cruelty in her eyes dampened features that might otherwise have been considered beautiful.

"I'm surprised to see it here," Abby admitted.

"Dad's sentimental that way. Despite what she did to him."

Abby ignored the goading remark. "Maybe he just views it as a piece of art. It's an incredible shot. Glamorous yet candid. When I was little, I thought Mother looked like a movie star in this picture."

Her stepsister's smile was cool and contemptuous. "I'm sure she thought so, too." She noted Abby's disapproving scowl and shrugged. "Eva was a vain woman. I don't have to tell you that."

Abby pounced before she could stop herself. "Was?"

Something dark and unpleasant glimmered in Lydia's eyes. "Wherever she is, she's older now. Age has a harsh way of crushing a person's vanity." Her gaze dropped to the photo on the console table. "I have no idea why he insists on keeping a shrine to her after all these years. What she did to him was unforgivable."

"Maybe we don't know the whole story," Abby said. "And I'd hardly call one photograph a shrine."

"Take a closer look. The matchbook in the bowl is from the restaurant where he proposed. The candle is her favorite scent. Need I go on? He adored that awful woman, though for the life of me, I've never understood why."

Her scorn rankled, particularly considering the circumstances. "That woman was my mother," Abby felt compelled to remind her.

"Was?"

Too late, Abby realized she'd fallen into a trap. She shrugged and muttered, "You know what I mean."

"I'm surprised you still feel the need to defend her, considering she discarded you as easily as she would last year's wardrobe."

No, she didn't. She was murdered. She may have planned to run away with her secret lover, but in time, she would have come back for me.

At least, it was comforting to think so.

"My mother is a topic you and I should probably avoid," Abby said.

"I would happily do so, but you're coming back here has not only stirred up a lot of bad memories, it's also raised questions. If we're going to work together for the next few weeks, we should clear the air once and for all. Stepsister to stepsister." As Lydia descended slowly, her derisive expression reminded Abby of the warning note thrown through her grandmother's window just the night before. *STAY AWAY.*

"What is it you think we need to clear up?" Abby asked.

Lydia paused at the bottom of the stairs, hand resting on the banister. "For one thing, you should know none of this was my idea."

"You mean my coming here? I would have been shocked to learn otherwise."

"My father is loyal to a fault. I'm not as forgiving. When you moved to Atlanta to live with your grandmother, you left him to salvage the business. It wasn't as easy as he made it look. There were a lot of challenges to overcome. Sacrifices had to be made. You were oblivious to all of it."

"I was seventeen years old," Abby said. "I was hardly in a position to run my own life, let alone a business. Besides, my mother left explicit instructions. She wanted James to have a place in the company for as long as he wanted one."

"Yes, and in catering to her wishes, he made

sure you were well taken care of, sometimes at the expense of everyone else. The company would have gone under years ago if not for his hard work. His and mine." Her eyes flashed. "All you've had to do is collect a check at the end of every year."

"I didn't make the arrangements, and no one has forced you to stay. But—" Abby took a breath and managed a conciliatory tone "—you and James have done a wonderful job. I do appreciate everything you've done to keep the business afloat. The very least I can do is help out while he recuperates."

Her stepsister moved into the foyer, brushing her fingers across the top of the console as if checking for dust. Or was she asserting her position in the household? "We're clearing the air, remember? All of this would go a lot easier if you'd just admit the real reason you're here."

"I thought I just did."

Lydia turned with a frown. "We both know what's really going on here. You're using Dad's illness as an excuse to insinuate yourself into the company. I'm not as trusting as he is. I knew it was only a matter of time once the company started to flourish that you'd decide to take advantage of our hard work."

"I don't need to insinuate myself anywhere," Abby said. "It's still my mother's company. But you must know by now that I have no interesting in taking over her business. I have a career. I'm happy in Atlanta."

"Would you be willing to put that in writing?"

"It already is. You have a contract, don't you?"

Lydia's mouth thinned. "Yes, and thank you for reminding me that I'm the hired help."

Abby suppressed an eye roll. "That's not how I meant it, and you know it."

"Perhaps not intentionally, but subconsciously, I think that's exactly how you meant it." Lydia picked up the photograph of Abby's mother and placed it face down on the table. "I remember the first time I stepped foot in this house. You and Eva let me know in a million subtle and not so subtle ways that I didn't belong here."

"That's not true."

"It is true." She walked her fingers across the back of Eva's photo.

Abby suppressed a shiver. She wasn't exactly afraid, but she was so unnerved by the look on Lydia's face that she found herself taking an involuntary step back. "It wasn't all one-sided," she said. "You never failed to let us know how much you hated it here. How much you hated us."

"How was I supposed to react? Just meekly accept whatever crumbs of civility you and Eva decided to toss my way? I had no choice but to defend myself. My dad was so enamored with you both that he didn't even notice his only daughter was being treated like an unwelcome guest in this house. It was three against one. Then Eva left and everything changed." An inscrutable smile played at the corners of her lips. "Dad and I still had each other, but you, the pampered princess, suddenly became the odd man out."

Chapter Seven

Abby was still a little shaken by the conversation, but she managed a smile and what she hoped was a pleasant demeanor as she carried the lemonade out to the veranda.

"I thought I heard voices inside," James remarked as he picked up his drink. "Did you find Lydia?"

"Yes, I saw her briefly in the foyer. She went back upstairs to make some phone calls."

"Was she able to answer your questions?"

"Uh, yeah. More or less." *She may even have revealed more than she meant to, in fact.*

James smiled. "You can also come to me if you have questions. I know Lydia can be a little prickly at times, but she's an invaluable asset to the company."

"I'm sure she is."

He leaned across the table and said in a low voice, "Can I make a confession?"

Abby nodded. "Of course."

"You've always resembled your mother, but

earlier when I saw you at the top of the steps with the sun shining behind you, I thought at first I was seeing a ghost."

"I didn't mean to startle you."

"It was a fleeting impression," he said. "And I meant what I just said as a compliment. Your mother was a very beautiful woman."

Abby was silent for a moment. "I can't help noticing how fondly you still speak of her. You don't seem to have the slightest trace of resentment or regret about what happened. How do you do that? You must feel at least a little bitterness for what she did." She watched him closely as she anticipated his answer.

He sat back in his chair with a sigh. "I did at first. I won't lie and say it was easy. It wasn't. But life is short. I made peace with the past a long time ago."

"Then you're a bigger person than I," Abby said candidly. "Her abandonment still affects some of my choices to this day. I don't know that I'll ever fully make peace with what happened." She picked up her glass but didn't sip. "You never considered divorcing her? You certainly had grounds."

"Divorce by default isn't always as easy as filling out paperwork or running a notice of intent in the local paper. There are a lot of steps to be taken and consequences to be considered. Besides, a part of me hoped for the longest time that she'd tire of her adventure and come back home. After a while, it ceased to be an issue."

"You never wanted to remarry?"

"Twice is enough for me, and anyway, Eva would be a hard act to follow."

"In more ways than one," Abby muttered. She glanced up. "I'm sorry. This is probably an upsetting conversation for you. Being back here has stirred up a lot of memories for me, but that's no excuse to invade your privacy."

"You're not upsetting me. I don't mind talking about Eva. In many ways, she was a remarkable woman. I understand your curiosity about her. You can ask me anything."

"Did you know she was seeing someone else?"

"I knew things weren't right between us." He shrugged. "The signs were there, I guess, but I didn't want to believe it."

"Did you ever find out who he was?"

"At one time, I thought I knew, but my assumption has been proven wrong."

She wanted to ask him to elaborate, but Lydia came out on the porch just then, and they both fell silent. Abby had a feeling she'd been listening in at the door and decided the conversation had gone on long enough.

"It's time for your medication, Dad."

"I'll come inside in a minute," he said. "Abby and I are having a nice visit."

Abby rose. "No, that's okay. You go do what you need to do. I'll come back another day."

He smiled. "Is that a promise?"

"Yes." To Lydia she said, "I'll see you at the office in the morning."

"Not tomorrow you won't. I'll be out of town for a couple of days." Her earlier animosity had either evaporated or—a more likely explanation—she'd put on a mask for her dad's benefit. She turned to him. "Remember, I told you that I have to be in Mobile first thing in the morning. Unfortunately, I'm also scheduled to meet our general contractor at the Moon Bay property on Tuesday. I hate to cancel, considering how overbooked he is and how much time has already been wasted, but I'm worried I won't make it back in time."

"That's an easy fix," James said. "Let Abby meet with the general contractor— Oh, for heaven's sake, Liddie," he said in exasperation when she balked. "You said it yourself. We need to get moving on those repairs. The season is almost over."

"I'm happy to help out in any way I can," Abby put in.

Lydia still wasn't convinced. "Are you familiar with the Moon Bay property?"

"I haven't been out there in years, but I know where it is."

James rose. "Lydia can tell you exactly what needs to be done."

She pursed her lips as she turned to Abby. "I'll need a guarantee that you won't let him talk you into unnecessary repairs or add-ons. And for God's sake, don't sign anything until I get back."

Abby nodded. "Got it. Do you have a list already drawn up?"

"I'll finalize the details tonight. I'm getting on the road early, so I won't be going into the office. I'll leave the paperwork and a key to the property here at the house. You can drop by tomorrow and pick it up. But don't come by too early. Dad needs his rest."

Abby glanced at James. "What time is good for you?"

"Any time after nine is perfect." To his daughter he said, "Stop fretting. Abby knows what she's doing."

"Just don't—"

"Sign anything," Abby said. "Got it." She smiled at James. "I guess I'll see you in the morning."

When she reached the end of the walkway, two things stopped her. She could feel a gaze on her back and turned to find both Lydia and James watching her from the veranda. Out on the street, the mystery man also tracked her from the gray sedan. Abby hurried to her vehicle, wondering again about his identity and intent.

TWENTY MINUTES LATER, she was back at the cottage. She'd called Wade from the road and asked him to meet her there. Letting herself in the front door, she dropped her bag on the floor and then crossed the room to glance out the back windows. She'd suggested he wait for her on the terrace, but he was nowhere to be seen. Was he running late, or had he decided to stand her up?

Annoyed and disappointed, she went outside and glanced down at the water. He was stretched out on the dock, an arm slung across his face, legs dangling over the side. For a moment, Abby was taken straight back to their high school years, back to those lazy summer days when she and Wade would spend hours on the water or lying in the sun, fingers entwined as they soaked up the heat.

She allowed herself the indulgence of those memories for only a moment before she started down the steps toward him. Halfway down, she paused to call out to him. He sat up and stretched, then threw her a lazy wave as he grabbed his shirt and got to his feet.

Their gazes met and held for the briefest moment before he pulled on the shirt, but the brief interlude was enough to flutter her stomach and stand her nerves on end. She took a breath and then another as he left the dock and started up the steps toward her. She waited for him to emerge from the oleanders and banana leaves before she spoke again.

"Thanks for coming."

He halted a few steps down and gazed up at her. He wore shorts and flip-flops, and his faded T-shirt had seen better days. If Abby didn't know better, she'd think he was one of the thirtysomething partiers who hit the lake every weekend, but she did know better. She'd done an internet search before leaving Atlanta. Wade Easton had grown himself quite a successful business.

"You sounded anxious on the phone." He moved up another few steps, his dark gaze raking over her. "Everything okay?"

Her hand curled around the guardrail. "I'm not sure. There was an incident at my grandmother's house last night. I don't know what to make of it."

"What happened?"

She swept her gaze over the lake. "Let's go up to the terrace first. We can sit in the shade while we talk."

Without another word, she turned and headed up the steps, glancing over her shoulder as she moved onto the flagstones. "Can I get you anything to drink? Water, tea… I think there may be a couple of beers in the fridge."

"Ice water sounds good if it's not too much trouble. It was pretty hot down on that dock."

Well, you were lying shirtless in the sun. "No trouble at all." She went back inside and filled two glasses from the ice and water dispensers in the refrigerator door. When she came back out, Wade had taken a seat at the wrought iron table.

She placed a glass in front of him and took a seat opposite him.

Instead of taking a thirsty drink, he wrapped both hands around the glass and ran his thumbs up and down the sides. "So, what happened last night?"

"Someone threw a rock through one of Grandmother's windows. It set off the alarm and the police came."

His thumbs stilled. "Was anyone hurt?"

"No, we're both fine, but my grandmother was pretty shaken up. We both were, to be honest. I'll get back to the broken window in a minute, but something odd happened earlier, just before the alarm went off. I woke up with a very strong sense that something was wrong in the house." She paused trying to figure out how to describe the sensation. "You know how it is when you return from a trip, and you get a strange feeling that someone has been in your place? Like the air has been disturbed or something? It was that kind of impression. Nothing tangible, just an inexplicable uneasiness. When I got up to check the house, I found my grandmother standing in front of the French doors that lead out to the back terrace. She said someone was in the garden."

"Could she tell who it was?"

"She said it was Mother." She waited for his reaction, but his expression never wavered. "Did you hear what I said?"

"I'm processing. Could she have been sleep-walking?"

"I wondered the same thing. She was acting very weird, but she seemed lucid. She said she had a dream about my mother before she woke up, and I'm sure she was still upset from our earlier conversation. I think she saw what she wanted to see. The thing is, she probably did spot someone in the garden. It was only a few minutes later when the rock came crashing through the front window."

He frowned, but his tone remained impassive. "You think this person was watching the house?"

"Why else would someone be in the garden in the middle of the night? It would certainly explain my uneasiness."

"What did the police say?"

"They seemed to think it was bored kids getting the same kind of kick they get out of smashing mailboxes. You know how those things go. They asked a few questions, wrote up a report and had a look around the house. They bagged the rock, but I doubt they'll find any prints. To be fair, at that point there wasn't anything more they could do. The perpetrator was long gone by the time they arrived. I didn't think it a good idea for my grandmother to be alone in the house, so I put her on a plane to Savannah before I left the city."

"That's probably for the best," he agreed.

"Have there been similar incidents in the neighborhood?"

"None that we know of, but I should probably tell you that the officers came to their conclusion without having all the facts."

"Meaning?"

She removed a baggie containing the note from her pocket and slid it across the table to him. "This was folded and taped to the rock."

He scanned the warning through the plastic protector. "Why didn't you give this to the police?"

"I had my reasons."

He glanced up in surprise, undoubtedly remembering her as the stickler for rules she'd once been. "I'd be very interested in hearing those reasons."

"I didn't want to frighten my grandmother. It seemed kinder to let her believe the act was random rather than targeted. Once I gave my abbreviated account to the police, I couldn't change my story without having to answer a lot of questions. I couldn't explain the note without telling them about my mother."

He scowled down at the paper. "A warning like this isn't something you'd normally want to keep from the police."

"I know, but the circumstances are extenuating." She reached over to retrieve the bagged note. "What could they actually do about it anyway, except check for prints and fibers? The likelihood of finding anything is pretty slim. Besides, we can do that ourselves."

That got his attention. "We?"

She hadn't meant to broach the subject of a partnership so flippantly. Better to find the right moment and then ease into the suggestion. Suddenly she wished for a good stiff drink rather than the ice water in her glass. She could be persuasive, but a little liquid courage sometimes helped. "I have something I'd like to run by you, but I'm not quite ready to discuss it yet."

"Now I think we have to discuss it."

"In due time."

He looked curious but didn't press. "Speaking of fingerprints, I don't need to point out that yours are likely all over the evidence."

"I took precautions. I put the note in a plastic bag as soon as I could, and I tried to handle only the edges of the paper. I know you think it was a mistake to conceal it from the police, but at least now I can compare it to handwriting samples at work."

"For a spur-of-the-moment decision, your rationalization seems pretty cogent." She couldn't tell from his tone if he was irritated or impressed. Maybe a little of both. "By handwriting samples at work, I assume you're referring to James and Lydia."

She nodded. "I can easily pull documents from

the files without anyone knowing, but I may not have to. Lydia is giving me a list of things to go over with a general contractor tomorrow at one of the properties. If I'm lucky, she'll include a signed work order."

He stared across the table at her. "You're completely serious about this, aren't you?"

"Why wouldn't I be?"

"The police haven't even had a chance to launch an investigation yet, and here you are going full throttle."

"It's a ten-year-old cold case, Wade. That's the reality. After the novelty of your discovery wears off, the file will get shoved into the archives."

"You don't know that."

She felt a flicker of anger at his stubbornness. "Maybe I don't want to take that chance. I'm not suggesting I interrogate witnesses or search private property. All I need at the moment is a handwriting expert. Can you hook me up or not?"

"I know a guy."

"Thank you." Abby sat back in her chair and tried to relax.

Wade waited a beat before he continued. "What if one of the samples turns out to be a match? What will you do then?"

"I'll take it to the police. And contrary to what you're probably thinking, I'm not completely naive. I know a match is a long shot. At most, it's a process of elimination. James is on the mend, but I doubt he has the strength to drive all the way to Atlanta and throw a rock through my grandmother's window. As for Lydia—" Abby thought about the possibility for a moment "—she's certainly capable, and she's made it crystal clear she doesn't want me around, but throwing rocks isn't exactly her style. She's always been a bit more cunning."

Wade slid his glass aside and leaned an arm on the table. "Long shot or not, let's play this out for a minute. Say it was Lydia or James behind the warning. How would they know you'd be at your grandmother's house? How would anyone know for that matter?"

"I've wondered about that, too," Abby said. "You were the only one I talked to about my trip. I didn't even let Grandmother know I was coming. And I assume you didn't tell anyone, either."

He looked almost startled by the suggestion. His posture remained relaxed with an elbow propped on the table and his long legs sprawled in front of him, but Abby sensed tension where none had been there a moment ago. The shift made her wonder.

"I didn't mention to anyone you were going to Atlanta," he said. "But I did tell my dad about the car at the bottom of the lake." He glanced at her. "I know we agreed not to say anything until the notifications had been made, but he was the police chief back then. I thought he might have some useful insights."

"Did he?"

"Not so far, but something may come back to him." He fixed his brooding gaze on the water. Abby took a long moment to study his profile, re-acquainting herself with features that were once as familiar to her as her own. She'd been obsessed with Wade Easton back in the day. The kind of intense infatuation that seemed exaggerated and ridiculous to her now, but back then, she'd been... what was the word her grandmother had used? *Besotted.*

She was a little embarrassed to remember some of those cringey moments and even more uncom-fortable with the knowledge that she still found him extremely attractive.

He turned and caught her staring at him. Her face colored as she glanced away.

If he noticed her discomfort, he chose to ignore it. He continued as if their conversation had never been paused. "There is the possibility that the warning doesn't have anything to do with your mother's death. Maybe James or Lydia wants to scare you away from the business. Either or both could have hired someone to follow you. That's how they knew you were in Atlanta."

She pulled out her phone and scrolled to the image she'd snapped earlier. "This guy was parked at the curb when I went by to see James a little while ago. I had the distinct feeling he was watching me or the house or both."

Wade picked up the phone and enlarged the image. "Pretty sure that's Detective Benson. I spoke to him at the lake yesterday."

"A cop? Do you think he was there to tell James about Mother?"

"It's possible. It's more likely he had the house under surveillance."

"If that's the case, he was being pretty obvious about it."

Wade shrugged. "Maybe he wanted to rattle some cages."

"He certainly rattled mine," Abby said.

He handed her back the phone. "Did James or Lydia see him?"

"I don't think so."

"Did they behave as if they already knew about Eva?"

"No, I'm certain they didn't know. James was in a good mood, and he seemed genuinely pleased to see me."

"Maybe that's what he wants you to believe. What about Lydia?"

Abby winced. "Not so pleased. But I'd be even more suspicious if she welcomed me with open arms." She twirled her ponytail into a bun and tucked the ends into the elastic band. "Investigations are a lot harder than I would have imagined," she said. "So many possibilities with so little to go on."

He gave her a quick grin. "Yeah, but my work wouldn't be nearly as much fun if everyone could do it."

"This is fun for you?"

His amusement vanished. "Not this particular case. Especially not this particular victim."

"I keep coming back to what you said about the spouse being the most likely suspect. Grandmother said the same thing, but neither of us could actually picture James as a killer. Lydia, on the other hand, had the added incentive of hating my mother. She hated me, too, for that matter."

"All the more reason why you need to be careful how you get those handwriting samples. You think the investigation is hard now, just wait. Once you start taking files out of the office or asking too many questions of the wrong people, alarms are going to get tripped. You need to remember that at the heart of this case is a cold-blooded killer."

She ran a hand up and down her arm where goose bumps suddenly prickled. "I know that. I'm not so naive as to think I can do this on my own. I work in real estate, for God's sake. Which is why I'd like to hire you to help me investigate."

"You want to hire me?" He looked at her as if she'd taken leave of her senses. Then he expelled a long breath. "Wow. That was unexpected."

She said awkwardly, "I know there's history between us. We didn't exactly part on the best of terms, but that was a long time ago. Who cares what happened in high school? Nothing matters to me more than bringing my mother's killer to justice. You're the one who found her car. You found her. Don't you have a vested interest in seeing this through?"

"It's a really bad idea," he said.

His resistance heaped humiliation on top of her embarrassment, but she pressed on. "Why?"

He sat up straighter as if preparing to flee. "I'm already working a case, and even if I weren't, I'm not that kind of investigator."

"Sometimes you are."

He lifted a brow. "How do you know that?"

"I went to your website," she said. "I even spoke with your assistant. She said you sometimes do private detective-type work for individuals if the money is right and the case or the client interests you."

"Did she also inform you of my rates?"

"She gave me a general idea. It's not a problem." Abby met his gaze without flinching. "I don't expect you to give me an answer on the spot. Take the night and think it over. We can talk again in the morning."

"I'm not saying I will, but if I did decide to take you on as a client, we'd need to establish some ground rules," he said. "No going rogue. No spur-of-the-moment decisions. No putting yourself in dangerous situations. You'd need to run everything by me before you acted. We'd do it my way or not at all. Could you live with those conditions?"

She answered without hesitation. "Yes."

"You say that now, but it may not be as easy as you think. I can be bossy and not always very tactful. I'd advise you to take some time to think about what you may be getting yourself into."

"I have thought about it. I came to you because you're the expert," Abby said. "I have no problem deferring to your knowledge and experience. But you're right, we should both take the night to think it over." When he started to get up, she said quickly, "Before you go… I need to ask a favor."

He sat back down. "Should I be worried?"

"I guess it depends on your perspective. I want to see the spot where you found the car."

"Why?" He looked slightly disconcerted by the request. "You won't be able to see anything unless you dive forty feet down, and I really don't think you want to do that."

She sat quietly with hands folded in her lap. "It won't make any sense to anyone but me, but I feel compelled to see where her car went down. I think it's a little like visiting a grave. The physical space is all you have left, and you cling to the hope that somehow there's still a connection. It probably sounds silly and maybe a little macabre, but if you don't take me, I'll just go out there alone."

He sighed and rubbed the back of his neck. "It's not silly. I get why you want to go, but we're running out of daylight. The sun will be going down by the time we get out there. Wouldn't it be better to wait and see how you feel in the morning?"

"Tomorrow is Monday. The police will have had all weekend to arrange for the necessary equipment to bring up the car. By morning, it could be too late. She might not still be there."

He searched her face. "This is really what you want?"

"Yes. And contrary to how it may seem, I'm in full control of my faculties."

He thought about that for a minute. "You impulsively withheld evidence from the Atlanta police, and now for whatever reason, you seem to think the two of us can solve a ten-year-old murder on our own. Sure. Sounds perfectly logical to me."

Chapter Eight

Abby cast off the lines and hopped down into the boat as Wade started the engine and reversed from the dock. He turned the prow toward the lake, puttering along until they were out of the no-wake zone before he pushed the throttle forward and trimmed the prop for maximum acceleration. Abby had been sitting in the back, but she moved up beside him as they zoomed across the choppy water, putting her hand on top of the windshield to steady her balance.

He glanced over, taking note of her profile as she stared straight ahead, her expression hidden behind oversized sunglasses. Her hair had come loose from the bun and flew about her face like strands of bronze and gold silk. She wore no makeup, and she didn't need any, though he doubted she would believe him if he told her so. It seemed to Wade that she'd always compared herself to her mother and came up lacking. Eva Dallas McRae had been a beautiful woman, but Abby was Abby. No comparison in his book.

She turned her head at that exact moment and caught him staring. Instead of glancing away, he met her gaze straight on, letting his attraction flare in his eyes and in a slow, easy smile. "Just like old times," he said over the engine.

An answering smile flashed before she turned to face forward. In that brief interlude, something changed between them. She'd let down her guard if only for a moment, but Wade wasn't so sure that was a good thing. Maybe his mother was right. Digging up the past did nothing but hurt the ones who had already been wounded.

He forced his attention back to the lake. With the setting sun, the weekend had officially come to a close. Most of the locals had already called it a day in order to rest up for Monday morning. The summer vacationers were still going strong on their Jet Skis and party boats, but the farther north they traveled, the lighter the traffic. The sun had dipped below the treetops as they approached the bridge ruins. Wade pulled back the throttle and put the boat in neutral as they rocked back and forth on the wake.

Unlike the last time he'd been there, the place looked deserted. No lake patrol, no dive boat, no police officers milling about on the bank. At the very least, a perimeter of ropes and buoys should have been set, but he knew only too well the limitations of a small-town police department. The current police chief probably thought it best not to call attention to the area until the car could be brought up.

After the wake settled, the boat sloshed gently in the water. Wade stood braced with feet slightly apart as he scanned the area with his binoculars. About five hundred yards upstream, something metallic sparked near the bank. His gaze had darted ahead, but he jerked his focus back to the spot, waiting another long moment before moving on again. Probably just a can floating in the shallow water near the bank, he decided.

He turned off the engine and allowed the silence to envelope them. The breeze brought the barest hint of smoke, the woodsy aroma stirring memories of campfires and cookouts. Beside him, Abby stood gazing around, too.

"It's so quiet," she said in a hushed voice. "Where are the police?"

"Not enough manpower, not enough resources. Take your pick," he said. "This isn't Atlanta. Small-town police departments are always spread too thin and this is the busy season."

She turned with a scowl. "Still, it seems strange they'd leave the area unguarded."

"Maybe it's for the best," he said. "A police presence would bring out the gawkers. Too many boats in the area could compromise the recovery operation."

"When do you think they'll bring her up?"

The significance of the pronoun wasn't lost on Wade. "Depends on how quickly they can locate the right equipment. The car is forty feet down and the bank isn't easily accessible. It's a tricky operation. They won't bring the remains up without the car," he added gently. "You'd risk losing whatever evidence might be trapped inside the vehicle."

"So we wait," she said.

"We wait," he agreed.

She took off her sunglasses and tossed them onto one of the rear seats as she lifted her gaze to the deepening sky. "It's spooky out here. Even the birds have gone silent. Did you notice?"

Her uneasiness matched his own. He rubbed the back of his neck as he scanned the water. He was reminded again of the meticulous research that had brought him to this spot in the first place. If someone wanted to get rid of a stolen boat, this would be a good location to sink it.

"Is this the spot?" she asked.

He pointed to the crumbling concrete braces on either side of the lake. "The car must have gone over several feet right of center. My dad said some of the guardrails were missing before the bridge was demolished. A car could have gone over the side without anyone ever noticing. Without safety barricades, that bridge was a tragedy waiting to happen."

He saw a shiver go through her as she hugged her arms to herself. "I can't stop thinking about what she must have experienced in those last few moments. The shock and panic as the car hit the water—the absolute terror as it sank and the water inside started to rise. She must have tried so hard to free herself from those handcuffs."

He took one look at her face and said, "I shouldn't have brought you out here."

Her arms tightened around her middle. "Do you think I wouldn't have those same thoughts back at the cottage? Or anywhere else, for that matter. It's all I see when I close my eyes. I keep asking myself, who could have done something that cruel to another human being? Mother was no angel, but she didn't deserve that. No one does."

He was careful how he responded. "It's possible she was unconscious before the car hit the water."

"Then why handcuff her to the steering wheel?"

"Maybe whoever trapped her wanted to make sure she couldn't get out of the car and swim to safety if she came to. Who knows what really happened? Ten years is a long time for a murderer to cover his or her tracks. You may never get all the answers you need."

"I refuse to believe that," she said. "My mother's killer was human, and humans make mistakes. All it takes is one clue, one lead, one witness to come forward to unravel the whole mystery."

Wade wasn't so optimistic. Or maybe a part of him was still afraid that his dad knew more about that night than he'd let on. Maybe he wasn't ready for the whole truth to be revealed. "We'll see what happens when word gets out."

Abby put a knee on the seat as she peered over the side into the water. He didn't need to be clairvoyant to know what she was thinking. Forty feet down, her mother's remains called out for justice.

While she stared down into the water, he once again lifted the binoculars. He scanned the bank where he'd seen the earlier flash. Maybe it was his imagination but he could have sworn he saw someone in the water. The person looked to be wearing a black wetsuit that rendered him virtually invisible among the shadows. As Wade continued to watch, the diver vanished underwater.

He swore and tossed the binoculars aside as he moved to the back of the boat and started pulling his dive gear from one of the compartments.

Abby followed him. "What are you doing?" she asked in alarm.

He was already checking his gauges. "Something isn't right. I'm going down to take a look."

"What do you mean something isn't right?"

He hauled on his harness and tank. "I just want to make sure everything below is the same as I left it."

She put her hand on his arm. "Stop for a minute. Tell me what you saw."

"I'm not sure," he admitted. "Could be nothing. I thought I saw someone with dive gear go underwater several hundred yards upstream."

She turned to glance past the bridge ruins. "I don't see another boat around. I didn't hear a motor, either."

"They wouldn't necessarily need a boat. They could have parked on the road and walked in from the bank. But like I said, it could be nothing."

Her hand was still on his arm. "What aren't you telling me?"

He didn't really want to spell it out, but he didn't want to leave her hanging, either. "Think about it for a minute. Supposing someone decided to compromise the remains before the police have a chance to bring up the car. A ten-year-old murder case will be hard enough to solve. Without a body, a conviction might be damn near impossible."

Her hand dropped from his arm as she stared at him aghast. "What do you mean by compromise the remains? *Steal?*"

He kept his tone impassive. "It's not likely. I'm erring on the side of caution. I've still got plenty of air in one of my tanks. It can't hurt to go down and take a quick look to put our minds at ease."

She gazed past him into the water. "What if someone *is* down there?"

"Then I'll chase them off."

She took another glance over the side of the boat. "I don't like this."

"It'll be fine. I'm an experienced diver."

"It's not your expertise that worries me. Whoever is down there may already have killed once before. Shouldn't we call the police?"

"How long do you think it would take for them to get out here? The damage could be done by then. I'll be fine." He nodded toward the bank. "See that stand of willow trees? Pull the boat underneath the branches while I'm down. The water is plenty deep even that close to the bank. Just raise the prop, and you shouldn't have any problems."

She still looked worried. "What then?"

"You wait. If you see another boat or a diver in the water, don't do anything. If they see you, get the hell out of here and call the cops. Otherwise, stay hidden until I surface. I'll give you a signal so you'll know it's me. Three waves over my head like this." He demonstrated. "I'll repeat in intervals until you see me. Got that?"

She nodded. "I still think we should call 911 and wait for backup."

"Says the woman who withheld evidence from the cops." He gave her a quick grin, trying to lighten the atmosphere. "I'll go down, have a look and then we'll know for sure that everything is okay."

He spent the next few minutes gearing up. Then he gave her a nod and a smile as he stepped over the back of the boat and balanced on the narrow platform to pull on his mask and fins. "Be back before you know it."

Fitting his regulator into his mouth, he gave her a thumbs-up and entered the water with a wide stride. As soon as he was under, he deflated his BCD and equalized the pressure in his ears. His light sparked off iridescent scales and bulging eyes as he descended into that strange, weightless world beneath the surface. Without the benefit of sunbeams filtering down through the water, his visibility was limited to a narrow path of illumination. His descent stirred up a cloud of sediment. He hovered for a moment until the particles settled before he began maneuvering through the bridge ruins.

Once more, he swam through gateways of rusted iron girders and around mountains of concrete and rebar until his light picked out the Rolls Royce Wraith sitting apparently undisturbed on the murky lakebed. He felt a momentary relief before the tomb-like silence engulfed him. He wasn't a superstitious person, and he didn't believe in ghosts or the paranormal, but as he swam toward the vehicle, he had the strangest feeling of being watched, of being tracked. He did a 360-degree turn in the water. Nothing amiss in any direction. Nothing out of place above or below him. Yet he couldn't shake off the same disquiet he'd experienced on the surface. Something was wrong.

He kept his light focused on the car as he swam up to the driver's side door and shined the beam inside the vehicle. The skeleton of Eva Dallas McRae floated behind the wheel, her empty eye sockets still searching for a destination that had eluded her for ten long years.

Observing the remains through the window seemed oddly intrusive and Wade started to move away when something whizzed past him in the water. He caught the movement out of the corner of his mask and thought at first a fish had darted by his cheek. In the next instant, he realized someone had launched a tiny missile from a speargun and the razor-sharp point was embedded in the corroded car door only inches from where he'd been a second earlier.

He was so startled, and he whirled so quickly that the light slipped from his hands. The beam hung eerily suspended in the water. He left it floating as he propelled himself toward the back of the car and hunkered on the lakebed. When no other assault was forthcoming, he swam up to grab the light and then circled the car, widening his search with each orbit.

At that point, he had no idea how long he'd been in the water. He checked his watch. Only twenty minutes had gone by, but he felt like he'd been under for a lot longer. Abby was probably getting concerned by now and may even have called the police. He searched for another few minutes, and then he inflated his BCD and surfaced.

The light was fading rapidly over the water. He wasn't sure Abby would be able to see him even with the binoculars, but he didn't want to call out to her. Sound carried over water. The last thing he needed was to alert his would-be assailant of his location. Or even worse, of Abby's.

Before he could signal a second time, he heard the boat engine start up. A few minutes later, she pulled alongside him, putting the shifter in neutral so that she could lend a hand as he hoisted himself over the side. Then she helped him shed his equipment as the boat rocked gently beneath their feet.

"What happened down there? You were gone for so long I started to panic. Another minute and I would have called 911."

He pushed his mask to the top of his head and sat down on the cushioned bench to remove his fins. "Someone shot at me. The spear missed me by inches."

"What?" She looked horrified as she crouched in front of him, her gaze darting over him. "Are you okay?"

"Yeah, I'm fine." He removed the mask and tossed it aside. "The line was cut. Which means it wasn't someone down there shooting at fish. They never intended to retrieve that spear."

She bit her lip in consternation. "How did they know you were down there? How could they even see you?"

Her hands were resting on his knees. He wondered if she even noticed. "They probably shot at my light." He finished with his gear and then, taking her hands, drew her up with him. "Did you see or hear anything? A boat, a car, anything?" He surveyed their surroundings as he cut the engine and listened to the silence.

"No, but my visibility was pretty limited behind those willow branches." She peered over the side of the boat as if she could spot someone still in the water. "Do you think they were trying to sabotage the car? I keep thinking about what you said earlier. That a conviction would be nearly impossible without a body. Is that really true?"

Before he could answer, a low rumble, like muffled thunder, rolled across the lake a split second before a geyser of water shot skyward several hundred yards north of them, just past the bridge ruins where he'd seen the diver. The shockwave that followed rocked the boat so violently they were almost tossed overboard. Abby clung to the rail, looking confused and terrified. Wade grabbed her and held on tight.

When the water finally calmed and the boat

stopped pitching, she said in a dazed voice, "What just happened?"

He grabbed the binoculars and searched upstream. The light was nearly gone by that time. He could barely make out what looked to be bits of debris floating on the surface of the lake. "Someone detonated an underwater explosive," he said. "You okay?"

She still looked stunned by the impact. "You think someone blew up the car?"

"No, the blast site is too far away. I'm going to go out on a limb and say someone just blew up Brett Fortier's stolen boat."

"Why?"

"My guess is, they already unloaded what they came for."

"By *they*, do you mean Brett?"

"Yes, but it's also possible someone else came looking for that boat. They probably got spooked by all the cops out here yesterday. They moved the cargo and then got rid of the evidence." He assessed her expression in the near dusk. "Are you sure you're okay?"

She stared back at him. "I'm fine. Are you? You're the one who was shot at underwater."

"Shot at, not shot. I'm good."

She drew a shaky breath and released it. "We seem to be dealing with some dangerous and desperate people, Wade. What do we do now?"

He scanned the area uneasily. "We get the hell out of here."

"Shouldn't we check the water to see if anyone is hurt?"

His response was blunt. "Do you really want to get that close? Your description of 'dangerous and desperate' seems pretty apt. If they have spearguns, they probably have other weapons, as well. We're unarmed, and right now, we're sitting ducks."

She nodded. "You're right. We shouldn't intervene, but we have to call the police. They should be out here, anyway. The area should never have been left unguarded."

Despite what he'd just said, Wade's first inclination was to get to the blast site before the cops arrived. The chance to explore the debris before the pieces were picked over and logged into evidence could have been helpful to his investigation. If he'd been alone, he would have done exactly that. But he wasn't about to take any chances with Abby's safety. If his suspicions were right, then whatever contraband had been hidden onboard had been moved ashore before the explosion. He remembered what his dad had said about the kind of people who might come looking for that boat.

He moved up behind the wheel and started the engine. "We'll call the police when we've put distance between us and whoever set those charges."

She came up beside him, but instead of balancing behind the windshield, she sat down and clutched the side of the boat. He wondered if she'd changed her mind about investigating her mother's murder. That first taste of real danger could be sobering.

Whipping the prow around, he pushed the shifter forward, and they shot across the water toward lights and safety.

A LITTLE WHILE LATER, Wade eased the boat alongside the bumpers on Abby's dock and turned off the motor. They both jumped out to tie off, and then she turned, her expression tense as she smoothed back her tangled hair. "What a mess."

"You look fine," Wade told her.

"You know that's not what I mean," she said in frustration. "I couldn't care less how I look. I'm talking about what just happened out there on the water. You could have been killed or seriously injured, and it would have been my fault."

"Your fault?" He frowned down at her. "How do you figure that?"

"I should never have asked you to take me out there in the first place. You didn't want to go, but I wouldn't listen. I all but badgered you into it." The night was warm and balmy, but she was still shivering.

He resisted the urge to put his arms around her and pull her into him. Hold her close until the adrenaline settled, and the shakes subsided. Instead, he tried to alleviate her guilt with a dismissive response. "First of all, nobody badgers me into doing anything I don't want to do. I can dig in my heels with the best of them. And second, I'm the one who found the car, remember? I'm the one who brought all this to your doorstep. So if anyone's to blame, it's me."

"I'm glad you came to me," she said. "I wouldn't have wanted to hear about Mother from a stranger."

"Regardless, I should have been more aware of the situation and our surroundings tonight. I knew the kind of people that would be out looking for Brett Fortier's boat. I also know Brett Fortier. Dangerous and desperate people do dangerous and desperate things. You didn't want me to dive, but I went down, anyway. So, no, none of this is your fault. Put that right out of your head."

They stood facing each other on the dock. Wade had the strongest urge to tuck back those tangled strands of hair and then take her face in his hands. Stare deeply into her eyes and promise her that everything would be okay. He'd make sure of it. But he continued to rein in his impulses because they were nowhere near comfortable enough with one another for that kind of intimacy. And because any promise from him would likely be meaningless to her.

"Wade?"

He shook himself out of his reverie and refocused his attention. "I'm sorry, what?"

"I asked what the police said when you called. I could hear a little of your side over the engine, but I think I was still too stunned to absorb it."

"I was patched through to Detective Benson. He's the one who took my statement yesterday after I found your mother's car, and I suspect he's the guy you saw earlier. He'll be lead investigator on both cases from here on out. I'm to meet him back at the blast site after I drop you off."

She said in alarm, "You're going back out there tonight? Isn't that risky? Whoever set those charges could still be lurking around."

"I doubt it. I'm sure they're long gone by now. But on the slim chance they're still in the vicinity covering their tracks, then a police presence is just what we need to safeguard the whole area. Not just the blast site but anything underwater that's evidence of a crime."

"The remains, you mean."

"And the car. It's a crime scene and needs to be protected. Forget what I said about gawkers. They're the least of our worries now. Hopefully, the necessary precautions will be put in place, but if not, I'll stand guard on my own if I have to."

"Not alone, you won't. If you stay, I stay."

The resolve in her voice impressed him. She'd been shaken earlier by the blast, but now she was ready to go back out there if and when he said the word. "Let's hope it doesn't come to that. We should both try to get some rest tonight. Benson wants both of us at the station tomorrow to give our official statements."

"What time?"

"I'll give you his number. You can call and set up an appointment before you go in. He'll probably want to talk to us separately."

"Why? He doesn't think we had anything to do with the explosion, does he?"

"It's routine. Nothing to worry about. Just tell him everything you saw and heard."

Her nod seemed absent, as if her mind had already strayed to other things. "What would have happened if you'd still been underwater when the charges were detonated?"

He told her the grim truth without the graphic details. "It wouldn't have been good. An underwater explosion transmits pressure with greater intensity over a longer distance. A shockwave that seems relatively mild on the surface can be deadly below."

Her voice turned solemn. "Do you think whoever shot at you with the speargun was trying to frighten you out of the water?"

"I guess that's one possibility."

She shook her head in disbelief. "I'm finding it hard to process all the things that have happened in such a short amount of time. You find my mother's car on the lakebed and discover that she was murdered. A day later, someone blows up a boat a few hundred yards away. You don't think the two things could be related?"

"Only in proximity. Like I said earlier, the police presence on the lake yesterday probably spooked someone into action. Any other connection is extremely slim in my book. But it's too early, and there are too many unanswered questions to rule anything out at this point."

She sighed. "We could stand here all night trying to figure things out, but you have a police detective waiting for you. Unless you want me to go back out there with you tonight?"

"No, get some rest. Tomorrow will be a long day for both of us."

"Tomorrow, I have to face Lydia," she said with an exaggerated shudder.

He smiled at her mild attempt to lighten the mood. "She won't stand a chance." He touched her arm briefly. "Come on. I'll walk you up."

"You don't have to. I'm fine now that my nerves have finally settled."

She didn't look fine. She still seemed jittery, and no wonder, after what she'd been through. Wade was still on edge himself, and the annoying ringing in his ears from the explosion was only now starting to subside. However, that was a mild irritation compared to what could have happened if he hadn't gotten out of the water in time. He'd likely be lying on the bottom of the lake with ruptured lungs and a bleeding brain.

"Humor me," he said. "I'd like to check things out for my own peace of mind before I leave."

She looked as if she wanted to argue his point but instead nodded and turned toward the cottage.

He followed her up the steps, and while she went through the inside of the house, he scoured the outside for breaches. They met back on the terrace.

"All clear," he said.

"Inside too."

He nodded toward the French doors. "Who has keys to this place besides you?"

"I assume there are spares at the office for the cleaning staff, painters, handymen and the like."

"You might want to think about changing the locks for the duration of your stay," he said.

"Oh, Lydia will love that added expense. But you're right. Better safe than sorry after everything that's happened. I'll pay for a locksmith out of my own pocket if she makes a fuss."

"Lydia never has to know. I can change out the locks myself. That is, if you trust me enough to loan me your key."

She went back inside, returning seconds later to drop a key in his hand. He didn't want to make too much of the gesture. Earning back her trust was never going to be this easy.

"Thank you," she said. "I feel like you're going above and beyond, and you haven't even agreed to take me on as a client."

"About that." He closed his fingers around the key. "I'm in."

She looked slightly startled and maybe a little apprehensive. "You don't have to say that because you feel responsible. What happened on the lake wasn't your fault. Don't let guilt or adrenaline make you agree to something you might end up regretting. Take the night and think it through."

He slid the key in his pocket. "I don't need to think. I've made up my mind."

"Well, then…" She sounded breathless. "What do we do first?"

"We'll strategize tomorrow after we've both given our statements to the police. Speaking of… I should get going before Detective Benson comes looking for me."

"Okay." When he would have turned away, she put her hand on his arm to stop him. "Wade?"

He waited.

She still looked tense, but there was a glimmer of something in her blue eyes that made his heart skip a beat as he stared down at her in the moonlight. He told himself to calm down, take it slow. *Don't do anything to scare her away.* "You wanted to say something?"

"Maybe now isn't the right time."

"Just tell me."

"I think if we're going to work together, we need to talk about how things ended ten years ago. Otherwise, it'll be hanging over everything we say and do."

Sooner or later, this conversation was bound to happen. He was a little surprised she'd brought it up so early, though. "You really want to open that can of worms tonight?"

"No, but I think we have to. I meant what I said earlier. It shouldn't matter what happened in the past. We're adults now. We've both lived our lives, and there are more important things to worry about than a high school breakup. But if I'm being honest, a part of me still resents you for what you did. I was pretty crushed by the betrayal, and I still don't understand how it even happened. Or why it happened. One day we were together, and the next thing I knew, you were with someone else. You said it yourself yesterday. Some people change but most don't. A part of me still wonders if I can trust you."

"You just gave me a key to your house."

"Because I *want* to trust you."

He took a moment before he responded. "I also said that things back then weren't always what they seemed."

"You did say that, but I don't know what it means."

"People made assumptions and I didn't correct them. I let them believe what they wanted to."

"Including me?"

"Especially you."

"Why?"

He scrubbed a hand down the side of his face in frustration, not knowing how to give a satisfactory answer while still holding back. "It sounds silly now," he said with no small amount of self-deprecation. "Silly and naive and probably a testament to how full of myself I was back then. I let you believe I was with someone else, because I thought it would be easier for you to leave town—leave me—and go live with your grandmother if we weren't together."

And because he'd been worried sick that his father had been planning to leave town with Abby's mother. Once he'd seen his dad with Eva, he couldn't look Abby in the eyes without wanting to blurt out the truth. He hated keeping things from her, but he had to think of his mother. Her mental health had declined significantly that summer. The gloom was so deep that some days, she couldn't even get out of bed. How far she might sink into the depression had been a constant worry for Wade. He would have done anything to spare her more pain. Even if it meant hurting Abby. He told himself it was best for everyone that she go live with her grandmother in Atlanta. He needed her gone and over him, because her absence made it easier for him to keep his dad's secret.

She searched his face. "Is that the truth?"

His hesitation was so infinitesimal, he didn't think she would have noticed. "Yes." But not the complete truth.

"That doesn't explain why you didn't come see me in Atlanta."

"Do you think your grandmother would have allowed it?"

"Once I turned eighteen, she had no say in the matter."

"By then, we'd both moved on. We were at different schools in different states. After a while, it seemed like high school was a million years ago."

She released a long breath. "Well, thank you for finally telling me."

Ten years too late.

"Wade?"

"I should go, Abby."

"I know." But instead of saying goodbye, she took his hand and tugged lightly.

Their gazes held for the longest moment before he bent and kissed her. She stood on tiptoes, placing her hands on his cheeks and kissed him back. He hadn't expected this. A part of him had hoped for it since the moment he'd spotted her on the terrace yesterday morning. But never in a million years would he have imagined she could feel the same.

They broke apart. Without a word, he turned and went down the steps to the dock, a decade's old secret still hanging between them.

Chapter Nine

Night had fallen by the time Wade returned to the blast site. Searchlights from the patrol boats raked over the dark waters while officers with flashlights combed the woods. He cut his engine and running lights and let the boat drift toward the shallows. Then he jumped down and sloshed through ankle-deep water to where Roy Benson waited for him on the bank.

The lanky police detective rocked a crew cut and an affable demeanor that belied his hardcore reputation. The spotlights from the lake reflected off his glasses, giving him an eerie, almost sightless appearance as he stood with hands in his pockets surveying the debris that had washed ashore.

"Seems like you have a nose for trouble, my friend."

"Just a run of bad luck," Wade replied.

Benson angled his head. "Let's talk over there."

They moved to a quieter area and spoke in low tones, mostly a repeat of what Wade had reported earlier on the phone. Benson didn't take notes. His questions were routine, but Wade had a feeling the detective listened intently to his answers so that he could pounce on any discrepancies. Wade knew how to play that game. He had a memory for minutia, and when he'd finished his second account nearly verbatim to the first, they both turned as one toward the water.

"I've seen a lot of out-there stuff on this lake, but underwater demolition is a new one," the detective said. "Boats usually explode on the surface when some fool sets off fireworks too close to the gas tank."

"Have you found anything in the debris to identify the boat?" Wade asked.

"The pieces that have floated up so far are pretty small. We don't even know for sure that it was a boat."

"What else would leave chunks of fiberglass in the water?"

"You've got me there." The detective skimmed his gaze over the lake. "Most likely you're right. We'll gather up what we can tonight and then send divers down in the morning to take a closer look. At least we haven't found any fresh bodies yet."

"I don't think you'll find bodies," Wade said. "Whoever set off those charges knew what they were doing."

"They?" Benson's voice sharpened as he gave

Wade a sidelong glance in the cast-off glow from the spotlights. Suddenly, he didn't seem so genial anymore, but the hard-nosed cop his dad had warned him about the day before. The same detective who had apparently been watching Abby outside her childhood home. "Why do I get the feeling you know more about this explosion than you're letting on?"

Wade braced himself, but he kept his tone even and his expression benign as they continued their awkward little dance. "I've told you everything I know."

"But you have to admit, the timing is pretty coincidental. You just happened to be in the exact area at the exact time when someone detonated underwater charges. You seem to have a knack for stumbling across unusual circumstances and events."

"Like I said, just a run of bad luck. Besides, I wouldn't call it that much of a coincidence. I've been looking for a stolen boat for days now. A boat your department didn't seem all that interested in until now," Wade added. "I had reason to believe it went down somewhere in this area. But you know that. I already explained everything to you yesterday when I reported the car with human remains inside."

Benson nodded. "You did say that, but I'm still a little unclear as to why you picked this particular spot to search."

"Sonar, aerial photography, common sense. Just take a look around, Detective. This part of the lake is remote. Hardly anyone comes back here anymore since they built the new bridge on the other side of town. You run out of gas or bend a propeller, you'd have to swim ashore and walk for miles. Perfect place to hide contraband on a sunken boat."

"Contraband?" Again, that sharp note in his voice. "You mean drugs?"

"Would that surprise you?"

"Nothing surprises me anymore. Superficially, we may seem like any other small town, but a place like this where strangers can come and go without being noticed attracts a certain element. You mix that with the casinos a few miles down the road, and you've got the makings of an underground criminal enterprise that could operate under the radar for years." He bent to retrieve a piece of debris from the water and examined it in the moonlight. "How well do you know Brett Fortier?"

Wade's reply was frank. "Not well. We went to high school together years ago. I can tell you that I wasn't a fan of his even back then."

"I heard you two used to get into it regularly. Over a girl, was it?"

Wade frowned. "Who told you that?"

"I asked around after we talked yesterday. An independent investigator hits town, we like to know what he's up to. Make sure he's not meddling where he has no business." Benson gave a low whistle to attract the attention of a nearby officer, and then he tossed over the chunk of fiberglass to be bagged and logged. "You had any run-ins with Fortier lately?"

"I haven't seen him since our high school graduation."

Benson feigned surprise. "I find that hard believe. His insurance company sent you down here to investigate what they believe to be a fraudulent claim. I'd have thought the first thing you'd want to do is get his statement on the record."

"I already have the signed police report and his insurance claim. I was hoping to keep a low profile for a few days while I searched for the boat."

"Didn't want to spook him?"

"Something like that."

"Too late for that now, looks like." The detective nodded toward the floating pieces of wreckage in the shallow water. "Can't keep something like this under wraps for long. The police activity out here for the past two days won't have gone unnoticed. As soon as we start moving in the heavy equipment to bring up that car, this area will be crawling with sightseers."

"Which is probably why someone blew up the boat."

"By someone, you mean Brett Fortier."

Wade nodded. "That's my guess. He salvaged

whatever he'd hidden onboard and then got rid of the evidence."

"Any idea where he's staying?"

"He's pretty elusive," Wade said. "If I were him, I'd try to stay somewhere close enough to keep an eye on things."

Benson scanned the darkness. "Plenty of rentals up and down the lake. Unless he checked in using an assumed name, we should be able to track him down."

"His sister still lives in town, but I wouldn't count on her being much help," Wade said. "She's pretty protective of her brother."

Benson scratched the back of his neck. "Let me ask you this. Do you think the explosion is somehow connected to the car you found?"

"I don't see how. Eva McRae disappeared ten years ago. The likelihood of a connection seems pretty slim to me."

"Maybe not as slim as you think. It's my understanding Brett Fortier used to work for her."

Wade shrugged. "He might have. She hired a lot of high school kids in the summer."

"How well did you know *her*?"

"I dated her daughter and she didn't approve. Beyond that, I didn't know much about her."

"You never heard her name connected to anything illegal? Rumor has it, she crossed paths with some pretty unsavory people in the early days of her business."

The detective's question jolted Wade even though the same thought had already crossed his mind. "I wouldn't know anything about that."

"Your dad was the police chief back then, right?" Benson's gaze narrowed as if he were trying to call up a forgotten detail. "He held the office for...what? Fifteen, sixteen years? He never mentioned anything about a money laundering operation? Some people think that's where Eva got the cash to buy up so much lakefront property."

"Her family is well off," Wade said. "I doubt she'd need to resort to a life of crime to finance a new business."

"But it's not just about the money for some people, is it?" Benson toed a can from the sandy bank. "They do it for the excitement. For the thrill of walking on the dark side. Does that sound like Eva McRae to you?"

"I was all of seventeen when she left town. I didn't do much analyzing back then."

"No, I guess you had other things on your mind." The detective's grin was quick and knowing. "I'll admit my theory is a long shot, but her involvement in the drug trade could explain why she made detailed plans to disappear without being followed. It could also explain how she ended up at the bottom of the lake."

"I don't know anything about that, either," Wade said. "As for my dad, he thought like everyone else in town that she left of her own accord. He had no reason at the time to suspect foul play. As you said, she made a lot of plans. Her husband and daughter found notes the next morning explaining her decision in her own handwriting."

"Yeah, but there's still something about her disappearance that I can't quite wrap my head around. Does it make sense that a law enforcement officer with Sam Easton's experience would buy a story like that so easily? Eva was a well-to-do woman with a thriving business and a devoted family, and she decides one day to throw it all away for a new boyfriend? And she leaves her husband and stepdaughter in charge of the company she built from the ground up? That's odd behavior any way you slice it."

"Hindsight is always twenty-twenty." Wasn't that what his dad had said the day before? "You have human remains inside a car. That's irrefutable evidence of foul play that my dad didn't have ten years ago."

"True enough. Let's focus on the daughter for a minute. The one you dated. Abigail, is it?"

"Abby."

"How did she get on with her mother? You said Eva didn't approve of your relationship. That must have caused a lot of friction, especially if she tried to break the two of you up."

"I never said she tried to break us up."

"That usually follows with parent disapproval.

What was the deal, anyway? She didn't think a cop's son was good enough for her daughter?"

Wade hesitated. "That was part of it, I guess. Mostly, she thought Abby was too young to be in a serious relationship."

"How serious were you?"

"We were in high school. Those relationships rarely make it past the first semester of college."

"But they can be pretty intense while they last."

Wade gave him a long stare. "Where is this going, Detective?"

"I'm just trying to get the full picture. Ten years is a long time. Details get forgotten. Disagreements get swept under the rug. I can't help wondering…did Abby have a temper back then?"

"What?"

"We've already established that a guy like Brett Fortier could push your buttons. What about Abby? Was she the type to lash out when someone angered her?"

"No. The opposite, in fact."

"She was the quiet type?"

Wade didn't need to be clairvoyant to intuit where this conversation was headed. They were entering dangerous territory, and he needed to watch what he said and how he said it. He'd come out here ostensibly to talk about the explosion. Roy Benson's attention had already reverted back to Eva McRae's murder.

"You're barking up the wrong tree if you think

Abby had anything to do with her mother's death. She was devastated when Eva disappeared."

"I'm sure she was, but there are any number of reasons why a teenage girl might be distraught in a situation like that. In my experience, guilt can be a debilitating emotion."

Wade stifled the four-letter response that sprang to his tongue even as he recognized Benson's tactic. He was trying to goad Wade into an unfiltered retort. "If Abby had been responsible, would she have gone to the police station and demanded an investigation?"

"She might if she wanted to throw off suspicion."

"You've got this all wrong," Wade insisted.

"Maybe, but it's early days in the investigation. I've barely scratched the surface. Plenty of time for new evidence to surface or eyewitnesses to come forward. Maybe we'll hear from the same witness who reported a dispute between Abby and her mother a few days before Eva disappeared."

Wade rose to the bait before he could stop himself. "What are you talking about?"

"You didn't know about the argument? I understand it got pretty loud and heated. The upshot was Eva threatened to send Abby to live with her grandmother if she didn't stop seeing you. That's a pretty powerful motive, wouldn't you agree? Especially if you factor in the potential of an inheritance that would allow her to go where she wanted with whomever she wanted." The detective seemed pretty satisfied with his conclusion.

"Who is this witness?" Wade demanded.

"An anonymous caller, apparently. We usually take those kinds of tips with a grain of salt, but Chief Easton thought it important enough to note in the file."

"What file?" The detective's fishing expedition had taken a turn that completely caught Wade off guard. He felt as if he were trying to pedal a bike with a broken chain.

"We'll get back to that in a minute," Benson assured him. "I still have a few questions about Abby."

"You're forgetting something pretty important about her mother's disappearance," Wade said. "If you really think Abby had something to do with Eva's death, then how do you explain away the handwritten notes that were left for her and her stepfather?"

"Yes, those notes are a puzzle," Benson agreed. "I'd be interested to know if a handwriting expert was brought in."

"All I know is that Abby had nothing to do with Eva's disappearance. She would never hurt anyone, least of all her own mother."

"So you keep saying." The detective tilted his head to study him. "You're pretty defensive of someone you dated back in high school. How close are you two these days?"

"Yesterday was the first time I'd seen her in years."

"When you went to tell her about her mother's car at the bottom of the lake?"

Wade figured it was pointless to deny it. "I didn't want her to hear about it on the news."

"Or maybe you wanted to make sure you two still had your stories straight after all this time."

"That's ridiculous." For the first time, Wade allowed a hint of outrage to creep into his tone. "Why would I report the car if I was involved in putting it down there?"

Benson commiserated. "Hey, I understand your frustration, but I'm just trying to do my job with what we have to go on so far. Even if you weren't involved back then, maybe Abby confessed to you after you went ahead and told her what you found. She spins her versions of events, and now you're protecting her."

"That didn't happen."

He shrugged. "Other theories will develop, and the suspect list will undoubtedly grow over the course of the investigation. One thing remains static, however. Someone killed that poor woman. Handcuffed her to the steering wheel and pushed her car into the lake. That's a rough way to go. Of course, we don't even know for sure the body is Eva's. If it turns out to be someone else in her car, then that's a whole new ball game. I was hoping to keep a lid on the investigation until we have the ME's report, but I guess that's out now that you've told Abby. You talk to anyone else?"

Wade had a feeling the detective already knew the answer to that question, or at least he suspected. Now was not the time to withhold information. "I talked to my dad. I thought he might have some insight into what happened. He didn't. He was as shocked as I was by the discovery of Eva's car."

"You sure about that?"

"Yes, I'm sure." Why did he feel as though he'd pedaled that chainless bike right into a minefield?

"Did you know he kept a file on Eva?"

"You keep talking about a file. *What* file?"

"Goes back to the time when she was still Eva Dallas. I've been reading through some of his notes. Pretty illuminating stuff. Do you think Sam would agree to consult on the case?"

His dad had kept a file on Eva? Why? "You'd have to ask him."

Benson nodded. "He could be a valuable resource given his history. I have to say, though, I'm surprised he never mentioned his interest in Eva. Seemed almost like an obsession. We all have cases like that in our careers. We know in our gut someone is guilty, but we can't find the evidence to prove it. We keep digging and digging until a single investigation becomes all-consuming."

Or until the obsession turns personal. "I'm not surprised he didn't talk about it," Wade said. "He rarely brought home his work. He didn't want to worry my mother."

"Or maybe he thought you'd run straight to Abby if you knew. He put a tail on her after her mother disappeared. I'm guessing you didn't know about that, either. Or did you? Maybe you had your own doubts about that girl. Maybe that's why the two of you broke up."

Wade had kept control of his emotions pretty well until that point, but he was finding it harder and harder to conceal his anger. Benson was like a dog with a bone. He wouldn't let up, and Wade was starting to feel the pressure. He reminded himself that was exactly what the detective wanted.

"Why we broke up is irrelevant and none of your business," he said.

Benson goaded him with a coy smile. "You know better than that. You're a cop's son. Ever since you found that Rolls Royce Wraith at the bottom of the lake with a corpse inside, everything about Eva McRae is my business. As far as I'm concerned, anyone she ever crossed paths with is a suspect. That includes family, friends, business associates. You. It most definitely includes Abigail Dallas."

ABBY HAD JUST climbed out of the shower when the doorbell rang. She wanted to ignore the summons. Just turn out the light and pretend she wasn't home. The day had left her exhausted, and she was still on edge from the explosion and Wade's underwater brush with death. And maybe still a little unnerved at how quickly things had escalated between them. She needed some quiet to think about that kiss and to analyze her emotions. Mostly, she just wanted to be left alone. The last thing she needed tonight was another visitor. But what if the police had come to question her about the events of the past two days? What if Wade had returned from the blast site with some new information? She drew on a robe and hurried down the hallway to answer the door.

Brie Fortier gave an exaggerated sigh of relief when Abby opened the door. Her blond hair was pulled back into a tight ponytail, highlighting her tense features as she breezed past Abby into the foyer. "You're home. Thank God." She took in Abby's robe and then craned her neck to see into other parts of the house. "I hope I'm not catching you at a bad time. You are alone, aren't you?"

"Yes." Abby combed fingers through her wet tangles, buying herself a moment to figure out what to say to her friend as she closed the door.

Her immediate worry was that Brie had heard about the car at the bottom of the lake. She had to be careful not to confirm or deny any of her friend's suspicions in order to allow the police time to make their notifications. Even though she didn't trust the local authorities to solve her mother's murder, she wanted to give the appearance of cooperation while she and Wade conducted their own investigation. This was the second time today she'd had to pretend not to know things, and she wondered if she'd be up to the task. Brie was nobody's fool, and Abby had never been any good at keeping secrets from her friend. She had a bad feeling the attorney in Brie would see right through her.

The doubts flashed through her head in a mere split-second as she assumed an expression of concern and mild curiosity. "You look upset. What's wrong?"

"It's Brett. I still haven't been able to reach him."

"You haven't heard from him all weekend? Is that unusual?"

"Not really. It's just... I can't get those sirens we heard yesterday out of my head. There's nothing in the local news about an accident, so where were all those police cars headed? I've been imagining all sorts of dire scenarios. I realize I'm overreacting, but..." She sighed. "You know me. That's what I do."

Abby took care with her response. "If those sirens had been about Brett, you would have heard something by now."

"That's what I keep telling myself." She gave

Abby a worried look. "You haven't heard anything, have you?"

"I haven't checked the news," she evaded. "I've been pretty busy all weekend."

"It's not like he hasn't done this to me before. He's always disappearing, and I sometimes don't hear from him for days or even weeks at a time. But that still doesn't stop me from worrying."

"No, of course not. When was the last time you heard from him?"

Brie furrowed her brow as she thought back. "He came by the house on Friday just as I was getting home from work. We talked for a bit and then he left."

"Did he say where he was going?"

"To meet some people for drinks."

"You don't know who he saw?"

"He was pretty vague. And before you ask, I don't know where he's staying. It's pretty sad, isn't it? I don't even know who my brother's friends are anymore, let alone any of his business associates. I don't have a single contact I can call to check up on him."

If Brett had the kind of business associates that Wade suspected, then keeping Brie in the dark was probably for her own protection. Her brother may well have been out on the lake earlier in the evening blowing up his own boat. He may even have been the one who shot at Wade with a speargun. All speculation at this point, but Brie had every right to worry. Her brother could be involved in a very dangerous business.

She said none of this to Brie, of course. Why upset her even more than she already was? "Doesn't he have a place on the beach? Maybe he invited his friends down to the Gulf for the weekend."

Brie was still frowning. "I suppose that's possible, but it still doesn't explain why he isn't taking my calls."

"Have you been to the police?"

"That's not an option," she blurted.

Her vehemence only stoked Abby's suspicions. "Why not?"

Brie tempered her answer with another shrug. "He hasn't even been gone that long. And like I said, he does this all the time. I should be used to it by now."

Abby didn't buy that excuse. Brie either knew or had a strong inkling as to what her brother was up to, hence her reluctance to involve the police. "What can I do?"

"Nothing. He'll turn up. He always does. I guess I just needed to let off a little steam." Brie paused, then said, "If I'm being honest, he's not even the reason I'm here. Not the only reason."

Abby tried to keep her tone and expression impassive. "Has something else happened?"

"I was hoping you could tell me." Something subtle shifted in Brie's tone.

Abby frowned. "What do you mean?"

"You said you'd call yesterday after Wade left, but you didn't. I've been on pins and needles all weekend trying to figure out what he wanted."

That was the reason she'd driven all the way out to the lake at nine thirty on a Sunday night? Abby tried not to sound impatient as she brushed off her lack of a follow-up phone call. "I guess it slipped my mind. I've had a lot going on this weekend, too. I'm trying to prepare for my first week in the office with Lydia. She'll be scrutinizing my every move, so I want to be ready."

Brie gave her a pointed look. "I thought you weren't worried about Lydia. You said you could handle her."

"I can, but putting in the extra effort never hurts. I've been going back through the quarterly financial records. Rental revenue is down this season and I've been trying to figure out why. But we don't need to get into all that right now." Abby tucked back her damp hair. "You really came all the way out here to talk about Wade Easton? You weren't seriously concerned for my safety, were you?"

"Not for your physical safety, but when you didn't call after you said you would, I started thinking something might have happened that you didn't want to talk about."

"Like what?"

She lifted a shoulder, but Abby had the impression she wasn't nearly as blasé as her mannerisms would indicate. "Maybe he brought up a bunch of bad memories or maybe he's trying to worm his way back into your life. I just hope you have the good sense to steer clear of him. Remember what I said yesterday. Once a cheater, always a cheater." When Abby would have protested, she hurried to add, "You can pretend all you want that a high school romance doesn't mean anything ten years down the road, but I was there. I know how badly he hurt you, and I know how long it took for you to get over him."

Abby thought again about the kiss on the terrace. She hadn't yet come to terms with the fact that she'd been the instigator or that the kiss had happened at all. The next logical step to resolving their unfinished business was suddenly an anvil hanging over her head.

"Well?" Brie demanded. "Am I right?"

"Give me some credit. Do you really think I'm that easily manipulated?"

"When it comes to Wade Easton? One word. *Kryptonite.*"

"You're relentless," Abby grumbled.

"That's because I'm very protective when it comes to my friends and family. I just don't want to see you get hurt."

Abby suppressed an impatient sigh. She didn't want to talk about Wade Easton or Brett Fortier or anyone else, for that matter. She just wanted to go to bed and get some sleep so that she would be fresh for her meeting with Detective Benson the next day. Apparently, she was already on his radar. The last thing she needed was to be so tired that she let something slip about the warning note she'd kept from the police in Atlanta.

"I appreciate your concern," she said. "But you're making a mountain out of a molehill. Wade and I barely know each other these days."

"Then put my mind at ease and tell me why he came to see you so early on a Saturday morning."

What exactly are you fishing for? Abby wondered. She hated having so many doubts about Brie, but the conversation was as troubling as it was bizarre. They'd managed to maintain a long-distance friendship since high school, but they hadn't been close enough in years to warrant this kind of overprotectiveness. What was the real concern here? What underlying motive had brought her all the way out to the lake when she could have easily called to get her answers?

They were still standing in the narrow foyer. The overhead light was on, and Abby used the opportunity to study Brie's features. Nothing gave her away on the surface. She always looked a bit stressed. Abby supposed it came from years of cleaning up her twin brother's messes. But something was different about her tonight. She wasn't just concerned. Abby could have sworn she'd spotted a flicker of fear when her friend's guard was down.

She leaned a shoulder against the door and folded her arms. "I have a question for you."

Brie's frown deepened. "What?"

"If you were really so worried about my meeting with Wade, why didn't you just call yesterday? Why did you wait the whole weekend to drive out here?"

"You've always valued your privacy, and I didn't want you to think I was being pushy or nosy. And, yes, I'm well aware of the irony of my barging in like this." She flashed a self-deprecating smile. "I was already brooding about Brett, and I got myself all worked up thinking I needed to come out here in person and check up on you." She glanced once more into the family room as if expecting to find Wade lurking in one of the corners.

"At least you realize when you're overreacting," Abby said.

"Yes, but it never seems to stop me. That's what happens when you go through life waiting for the next shoe to drop." She was starting to sound like the old Brie, a prickly combination of pragmatism, fatalism and anxiety topped with a large dollop of self-awareness. "My doctor says I may be getting an ulcer. An *ulcer* and I'm not even thirty yet. Ouch." She flattened her hands on her stomach and winced.

"Are you okay?"

She closed her eyes on a deep breath. "I will be." Another breath. "You're being awfully patient with me. I can't imagine what you really think about me showing up at your door so late and babbling on about things that are none of my business."

"I think this is all camouflage," Abby said. "You've got something else on your mind. You don't know how to bring it up, so you keep dancing around the real issue."

Brie instantly sobered. "Anyone ever tell you that you missed your true calling? As a matter of fact, there is something else I'd like to talk to you about. I'm not sure how you'll take it, though."

"Then maybe we should go inside and sit down." Abby waved her into the family room.

Brie stalled for a bit. "Are you sure? I know it's getting late, and we both have work tomorrow. Luckily, I only have to deal with an irate client and a possible lawsuit. You have to face Lydia."

"She's not as bad as we make her out to be."

"Yes, she is." Brie was still clutching her stomach. "She's worse, in fact."

As soon as they moved into the family room, Brie dropped the subject of Abby's stepsister and went straight to the windows to peer out into the darkness. For the longest moment, she seemed lost in thought as a strange sort of energy crept into the room. Something was definitely going on with her. Despite those flashes of the old, fretful Brie, a deeper moodiness hung over her tonight, along with an air of uneasiness that seemed almost tangible. Earlier, Abby had attributed the flickers of darkness in her friend's eyes to an inexplicable fear, but now the emotion permeating the room seemed more like dread.

What do you know that you're not telling me?

Abby suppressed another shiver as she thought back to some of their conversations over the years and how Brie would so often bring up Wade's name as a subtle, repetitive reminder of his betrayal. Was it possible she had unrequited feelings for Wade? That would certainly explain her unusual behavior tonight and her near obsession with what had transpired between Abby and Wade. Maybe she really did need to get something off her chest.

"Brie?"

Without turning, she said, "I've always loved this cottage. I tried to buy it once. Lydia said it couldn't be done without your signature, and I knew you'd never part with it."

"You tried to buy my cottage? Why?"

"The view, the location. It's the perfect place. I didn't think you'd ever come back to the lake, and it seemed a shame to waste all this charm on renters." She turned. "But here you are."

Of all the properties her mother had ever owned, the cottage was the only place to which

Abby had ever felt a real connection. She didn't know how she felt about Brie's revelation. There were dozens of houses up and down the lake. Why this place specifically?

Abby tried to shake off her disquiet as she motioned to the sofa. "Why don't we sit? Tell me what's going on with you tonight."

"That's a long story." Brie perched on the edge of the sofa like a bird waiting to take flight.

"You wanted to talk, so let's talk." Abby sat down in a chair facing the sofa and curled up her legs.

Brie clasped her hands in her lap and met Abby's gaze with a hint of defiance. "It's about Wade."

Abby said in disbelief, "*Still?* Haven't we exhausted that subject?"

"Not quite. Please, just hear me out. It's not only about yesterday morning, though his showing up out of the blue was certainly the catalyst. I feel I haven't properly expressed the depth of my concern. I know this is none of my business, but you're my best friend and there are things you need to know. Things I've heard over the years."

"About Wade? What things?"

"He's very ambitious. Driven, one might say."

"That's not a crime," Abby said. "Some might consider it an attribute."

"And others like me might consider it a pitfall. I saw the way he looked at you yesterday and the way you looked at him. It was like high school all over again, except the stakes are much higher now. Besides your trust fund and your future inheritances, you've become successful in your own right. I'm willing to bet he has a pretty good idea of how much you're currently worth."

Abby sat stunned. She hadn't expected that. "You think Wade is after my money?"

"I think he's always been after your money," Brie replied bluntly.

"Well, thanks. It's not like anyone could want me for myself."

"You know that's not what I mean. He's attracted to you. Anyone can see that, but I can't help wondering why he made a beeline to the cottage the moment he learned you were back in town."

"You're wrong about him." Since when did she feel the need to leap to Wade Easton's defense? He was a grown man. He didn't need her or anyone else protecting his honor. And, anyway, he'd probably find the whole conversation more amusing than offensive.

"If I'm wrong, then why are you so evasive about what went down between you two yesterday morning?"

Abby said coolly, "Maybe your instincts were right. Maybe it's not something I want to talk about."

"Or maybe you just don't want to talk to *me*

about it. Is that it?" She pursed her lips in disapproval. "The only other reason your evasiveness makes sense is Brett. Wade wanted information about my brother." She leaned forward. "What did you tell him?"

"I didn't tell him anything because I don't know anything." Abby was still trying to get a handle on Brie's peculiar behavior, the way she kept slipping from one subject to another but always coming back to Wade.

Maybe Abby was the one overreacting, but her mother's murder was starting to color her every conversation and interaction. She couldn't help questioning motives or searching for flickers of guilt. Fairhope was a small town. It wasn't a stretch to think the killer might have been someone both she and her mother had known. But Brie? They were the same age. Abby found it hard to imagine a seventeen-year-old luring Eva out to the bridge and then getting the jump on her.

"I don't understand why you think that he'd think that I'd know anything about Brett," she said. "I just arrived a couple of days ago. I didn't even know his boat had been stolen."

"You and I were best friends in high school. Inseparable until Wade came along. Why wouldn't he assume that I'd confide in you?"

"But you didn't."

"Because there's nothing *to* confide, but he doesn't know that. You know how he's always felt about Brett. Ever since you went out with my brother—"

"We didn't go out. We had one date," Abby hastened to clarify.

"One or a dozen, what does it matter? Wade never forgot and he sure as hell never forgave."

"There was nothing to forgive. He and I weren't even a couple then."

"Tell that to Wade."

Now it was Abby who leaned forward. "Tell me the truth, Brie. Is Brett in some kind of trouble?"

A mask immediately dropped. "Why would you ask that? What did Wade tell you?"

"I just don't think an insurance company would go to the expense of hiring a fraud investigator if they believed Brett's claim was on the up-and-up."

"Has Wade gone to the cops?"

Abby blinked in confusion. "About the boat?"

"What did he tell them?"

"You'd have to ask him." Were they even still talking about a stolen boat? "You never answered my question."

Brie dismissed the query with a wave of her hand. "Insurance companies are notorious for denying claims. They don't need to prove fraud to renege on a policy. But if they're looking to make an example out of my brother, they certainly picked the right investigator to dig up dirt. If Wade can't find anything, he'll just make something up."

"He wouldn't do that," Abby said. "He takes his job seriously. And I doubt he's been holding a grudge against Brett since high school."

Brie stared at her in silence. "Well, that didn't take long."

"What?"

"All these years in the cutthroat business of commercial real estate, and you're still as naive as you were at seventeen when it comes to Wade Easton."

"I may not be as naive as you think," Abby said. "And I notice you *still* haven't given me a straight answer."

Anger flared in Brie's eyes before she glanced away. "Brett is no angel. I'll be the first to admit he's had his troubles over the years, but his past in this matter is irrelevant."

"If that were true, you wouldn't feel the need to cover for him. I think you came here to find out if Wade has managed to connect all the dots."

Brie went absolutely still. For a moment, she seemed to hold her breath. "What dots?"

"Why did Brett bring that boat up here in the first place? Was he running from someone? Hiding from someone? What's he involved in?"

It didn't make any sense, but the look that flashed across Brie's face almost seemed like one of relief. She hid the fleeting emotion behind a guise of hurt feelings. "That's not my friend talking. That's Wade Easton talking."

"No, it's me," Abby assured her. "You came over here looking for answers. You must have known your questions would make me curious."

Brie stood abruptly. "This was a bad idea. I can see he's already started to turn you against me. Just like he tried to do in high school."

"Wade has never said a bad word against you to me."

"No, he's a little more subtle than that. He uses my brother to come between us."

"You're the one who keeps bringing Brett into the conversation." Abby untucked her legs and slowly rose. "Your brother's stolen boat doesn't concern me. What I can't figure out is why you keep trying to involve me."

"That's not what I'm doing."

"Why did you really come here tonight? What aren't you telling me?"

Brie started for the door. "Maybe you should ask Wade that same question."

Abby followed her into the foyer. "If you've got something to say, just spit it out."

She whirled. "Did you know your grandmother paid him to stop seeing you?"

Abby was taken aback. "What?"

"That's what I heard. He took money from your grandmother, and then he started seeing someone else. He was paid to break up with you."

Abby didn't believe a word of the accusation, and yet… "That's not true."

"Ask him. He's good at keeping secrets. Before you get too involved, maybe you should find out what else he's been keeping from you all these years."

The look in Brie's eyes sent a chill straight through Abby's heart. Then she opened the door and disappeared into the night.

Abby stood staring after her, wondering what on earth had just happened. Brie had always been protective of her brother, but this was different. Something had changed in the short time since Abby had last seen her. Yesterday morning, Brie's warning about Wade had seemed almost rote. Tonight, her attack had turned vicious.

She glanced out the sidelight, then moved to one of the front windows that had a view of the street. Brie was already backing out of the driveway, but then she braked, and a split second later, someone emerged from the bushes and got into the car. The dome light flashed on, illuminating a man's profile. The headlights were turned off and the security lights around the cottage didn't penetrate the tinted windows. Brie and her companion sat in the dark for a few minutes before the dome light flashed again.

The man turned to stare at the house as he emerged from the vehicle. For a split second, his gaze seemed to connect with Abby's through the glass. She gasped and jerked back from the window. When she chanced another glance, Brett Fortier had already vanished into the shadows.

Chapter Ten

Abby tossed and turned for the longest time, unable to get that strange conversation with Brie out of her head. She didn't want to believe the accusations about Wade, but like it or not, a nerve had been touched. How much did she even know about him these days? Or about Brie, for that matter. They'd kept in contact after Abby had moved to Atlanta and had seen each other on occasion, but they were no longer close. Tonight, she'd seemed almost like a stranger.

On and on Abby's thoughts churned until she finally fell asleep only to startle awake sometime later with the terrifying notion that she was no longer alone in the house. Heart pounding, she peered into the dark and listened to the quiet.

A soft rustling sound came to her, followed by a faint breeze. She told herself it was just the air conditioner. She'd checked all the locks after Brie left. Knowing that Brett Fortier might be lurking outside had made her especially cautious. She thought about calling Wade, but Brie had successfully planted a seed of doubt. Come morning, she might be able to see things more clearly, but tonight she was on her own. If someone was in the house, she'd have to deal with the intruder without any help from Wade Easton.

The sound of stealthy footsteps in the hallway froze her. Her gaze darted about the room, searching frantically for a weapon even as the sound faded, leaving her to wonder if she'd imagined the footfalls. Maybe she was still half asleep, experiencing something she'd read about called a waking dream.

She lay perfectly still for a moment longer before throwing off the covers and swinging her legs over the side of the bed. Then she opened the nightstand drawer and removed the heavy flashlight that had been placed there by a previous guest. Gripping the metal in one hand and her phone in the other, she rose and tiptoed to the doorway, glancing both ways down the hallway before venturing out of the bedroom.

It was a cloudy night. No moonlight to guide her, but she didn't dare turn on the flashlight. Not yet. Not until she could convince herself she was alone with only her imagination. Her waking dream.

Down the hallway she crept, past the other bedroom and a bathroom and into the family room. Nothing seemed amiss at first. No lurking shadows. No more stealthy footfalls. Yet the very air seemed charged as if negative energy lingered from a prowler.

Her fingers tightened around the flashlight as she inched into the room, her gaze roaming ahead of her, searching every darkened corner until the rustling sound came to her again, follow by a wispy breeze that stirred her hair.

A gauzy curtain floated ghostlike in the draft. She stared at the movement in bewilderment until she realized one of the French doors had been left open. Her initial reaction was one of relief. That explained the rustling sound. Then she reminded herself she'd checked the doors before retiring. Someone had come into her house while she slept and left by way of the terrace. Or were they still inside?

Her instinct was to make a dash for the bedroom and lock herself inside, then call the police. She did none of those things. As she stood searching the darkness, anger momentarily nudged aside her fear. First her grandmother's home in Atlanta had been vandalized, and now someone had invaded her private space at the lake.

Holding up her lit phone, she said into the darkness, "If you're still here, I've already called 911. The police will be here at any moment now."

As if on cue, a siren sounded in the distance, unrelated to her circumstances, but the intruder wouldn't know that. She held her breath and waited. Nothing stirred save for the curtain. After several long moments, she decided she really was alone. Keeping her phone at the ready, she hurried over to the French door and stepped out on the terrace. The stairs to the dock lay in deep shadow, and the water below looked dark and menacing, with only a faint shimmer on the surface.

Somewhere out on the lake, an engine fired up. She listened to the putter until the driver hit the throttle and the sound hit a crescendo, then faded. As she turned back to the door, part of the conversation she'd had earlier with Wade came back to her.

Who has keys to this place besides you?

You might want to think about changing the locks for the duration of your stay.

Lydia never has to know. I can change out the locks myself. That is, if you trust me enough to loan me your key.

Now Abby really was letting her imagination get the better of her, she decided. She straightened her shoulders and gave herself a pep talk as she went back into the house and locked the door. Then she turned on all the overhead lights as she made the rounds through the rooms.

The envelope with her name scrawled across the face went unnoticed until she returned from the back of the house. Someone had left a note for her on the kitchen island. She reached for the envelope and then jerked back her hand, realizing she needed to be more careful about prints.

Rummaging underneath the sink, she found a pair of cleaning gloves and slipped them on before removing the note and scanning the brief message: *YOU WERE WARNED.*

FROM HIS STAKEOUT spot on the bank, Wade shifted his position to alleviate a cramp in his calf. He'd been hunkered in the bushes for hours, it seemed. He glanced at the clock on his phone. Just after one in the morning. Already Monday. Going on two days since he'd found the car at the bottom of the lake, and Eva McRae's murderer still roamed free. He could picture her down there now, trapped and waiting restlessly for justice.

Detective Benson had said arrangements were underway to bring up the vehicle, though he'd been vague on a time line. Possibly in a matter of hours, the skeletal remains would be on the way to the morgue, where the ME would compare the teeth and bones to Eva's dental and medical records.

If the results were inclusive, then Abby would be asked to submit a DNA swab. Either way, they'd soon know if her mother was the murder victim or if someone else had ended up in her car at the bottom of the lake. That would certainly complicate an already multifaceted investigation. Once the remains were identified, the question on everyone's mind would be the same as it had been ten years ago. Where was Eva Dallas McRae?

Wade's boat was well hidden by the willow branches, and the moonless night helped conceal him from prying eyes on either side of the lake. Earlier, he'd pretended to head back to town when the police left, but once out of sight, he'd doubled back. Detective Benson had agreed the area needed protecting, but the best he could promise was a drive-by patrol for the rest of the night. A squad car up on the road could too easily be eluded by someone with malicious intent. A diver could either hide a boat in the shadows near the shoreline as Wade had done or enter the water from the bank. The same kind of demolition used earlier to destroy a sunken boat could also obliterate Eva McRae's car and the evidence that remained inside.

Rummaging in his backpack for his night-vision scope, he scanned the trees on the opposite shore. He could just make out the trail that led up to the old highway. A similar trail remained on his side of the lake. The original road had been bisected by the demolished bridge, and each section was now a dead end. Without water or ground traffic, the isolated area was the perfect place to conduct nefarious business.

Time dragged as he listened to the sounds of the lake and the surrounding woods. The cicadas were loud tonight and almost as incessant as the mosquitos that buzzed around his face. He lifted a hand to swat them away as the sound of a car engine came to him through the trees. The roar grew louder as high beams swept over the empty space where the bridge used to be. The engine died and the headlights went out. A moment later, a car door closed with a soft thud. In the ensuing silence, Wade adjusted his position so that he had a better view as he followed the path up the embankment with his scope. He could see someone at the top facing the water.

He returned the scope to his backpack and then slipped from his hiding place to inch up the embankment, inwardly cursing at the soft crunch his footfalls made in the underbrush. He hoped the person at the top would attribute the sound to a night creature stirring. He also hoped they were unarmed.

The moon peeked briefly from behind a cloud, the sudden illumination both a blessing and a curse. He stayed crouched, using the shadows for cover as he crept closer. If the moonlight would just hold for a few seconds longer, he'd be able to see who was at the top of the bank and what they were up to.

Whether alerted by a sound or instinct, she turned. Wade could have sworn his mother's gaze met his in the split second before a cloud drifted back over the moon and the shadows once again veiled her features.

He held his position, stunned and unwilling to believe his own eyes. For a moment, he thought about calling out to her. What was she doing out here alone at this time of night? Terrible thoughts raced through his head. A parade of unbearable visions. He had to remind himself that she was better now and had been for a long time. She was painting again and seemed happy. She wouldn't hurt herself. She would never bring that kind of pain to a husband who loved her and to a son who had dedicated himself, even at the age of seventeen, to her protection.

Shaking off his own gloom, he edged closer until he could make out her silhouette even without the benefit of moonlight. She stood perfectly still as if listening to the night. Or as if the shock of their brief encounter had rendered her motionless.

Had she really seen him? Should he approach and make sure she really was okay? Or would she prefer that he vanish back into the woods and forget he'd seen her out here?

Something came to him as he watched her. She wasn't so much frozen in shock as she was mesmerized by the water.

Another thought followed. *She knows.*

Maybe his father had told her about Wade's discovery at the bottom of the lake, or maybe she'd overheard them on the deck before they'd relocated to the dock. Why else would she drive out here in the middle of the night to stare at the water? Of all the places on the lake, why *here*?

Yes, she knew.

About the car. The affair. All of it.

She knew…but for how long?

He followed her gaze to the water as a deeper dread descended. He couldn't allow those dark thoughts to morph into images. He wouldn't let his questions turn into suspicion. His mother was a gentle soul. She wouldn't hurt a fly, let alone a human being. There must be a reason she'd driven out to this particular spot in the middle of the night, and Wade told himself he should make his presence known and ask her. He didn't. He couldn't. *Maybe some secrets are best left buried.*

When he returned his gaze to the top of the embankment, she was gone. He'd lost her in the darkness. Crouching in the bushes, he listened for sounds of her departure. Nothing came to him. He could only assume she was still up there somewhere, but he could no longer see her. He felt weighed down by that heavy trepidation even as the whole scene struck him as surreal. Dream-like. He could never have imagined in a million years that his search for a stolen boat would lead him here. That he would find himself hiding in the dark from his own mother.

He felt almost relieved when he finally heard the soft bump of the car door, and a moment later, the engine fired up. The headlights beamed out over the water and then arced through the trees as she turned her vehicle and headed back the way she'd come.

Now a new question niggled. Should he call his dad and let him know she'd left the house? Was his dad already pacing the floor, worried where she'd gone, and if and when she'd come home?

Wade decided he'd call as soon as he made it back to the boat. He was so focused on what he would say to his dad and what his mother's trip to the lake meant that he failed to take note of the sound of a stealthy tracker. A twig snapped behind him, but his senses and reflexes were still dulled by shock.

Before he could turn or deflect, he was struck at the back of his head with a blunt instrument. The pain barely registered before he hit the ground facedown, and everything faded to black.

WADE OPENED HIS eyes to darkness and a loud ringing in his ears. He had no sense of where he was or what had happened. For a moment, he didn't even know his own name. But he was acutely aware of two things: a sharp pain at the back of his head and a rocking motion that made his stomach churn. He lay on his back staring up at the ceiling. He blinked and saw a light above him. He blinked again and willed away the cobwebs. Not a ceiling but the sky. Not a light, but the moon cloaked in wispy clouds.

Swallowing back the nausea, he tried to sit

up, groaned and collapsed, putting a hand behind his head to cushion the blow. Taking several deep breaths, he tried again, grabbing onto the first thing he could find and heaving himself up to a sitting position. He looked around and saw nothing but water. Slowly, his predicament penetrated his fuzzy brain. He was adrift in the middle of the lake.

He glanced around for his backpack. His boat key was inside, along with his cell phone and the night-vision scope and—

What was that noise?

As his head cleared and his senses sharpened, he realized the resonance in his ears was, in fact, the muffled ringtone of a cell phone. He followed the sound to the back of the boat and lifted one of the bench seats. He fumbled in the dark with the unfamiliar phone before he managed to accept the call.

A male voice instantly responded. "Get off the boat."

"Wha—"

"An explosive device with a remote detonator has been placed underneath one of the seats. Don't bother looking for it. You've got less than two minutes to make it to shore."

Wade didn't waste time with questions or a search. He dove over the side of the boat and swam for all he was worth. Once he could feel the sandy bottom beneath his feet, he rose and sprinted through the shallow water to collapse on the bank. A split second later, a plume of sparks shot skyward, exploding into a shower of colorful stars that rained down upon the water.

Not a bomb but fireworks. Set off by a remote firing system.

Cruel joke. Somebody having a little fun at his expense.

Wade was relieved and ticked off at the same time.

He watched as the last sparks sizzled out on the surface, and then he scrambled up the embankment and made his way back to where he'd been ambushed. His backpack lay on the ground where he'd dropped it. His phone was still inside, the ringtone already pealing.

The same voice said, "It could have been a bomb."

Wade glanced at the caller ID: Number Unavailable. Then he searched the darkness all around him. Someone was obviously watching him, possibly using his own night-vision scope to track him.

"Who is this?"

"The guy you've been trying to shaft out of a quarter of a million dollars."

"Brett Fortier."

The caller gave a low laugh. "Sorry about the bump on your head, but I needed to get your attention."

"Well, you have it," Wade said. "What do you want?"

"You need to back off, buddy. You're bringing a lot of scrutiny to the area—to *me*—and that's bad for business. Not to mention my health."

"What business would that be?"

"The kind that doesn't concern you."

"I disagree," Wade said. "You made it my concern when you tried to kill me."

"Actually, I probably saved your life."

"You'll understand if I have a hard time mustering my gratitude." Wade continued to skim the area, looking for a telltale flash of light at the top of the embankment or a sudden movement in the trees. "What was on the boat before you blew it up?"

"See, questions like that are just going to get you in trouble. But for old time's sake, I'm willing to cut you some slack if you agree to keep your mouth shut. It'll all be over in a couple of days, anyway."

"What will?"

"Walk away, Wade."

"You know I can't do that."

The affable tone vanished. "Then consider yourself warned."

Chapter Eleven

Abby rose early the next morning, exhausted from stress, fear and lack of sleep. Wade texted while she was having coffee on the terrace. He wanted to know when he could come by and change the locks. Securing the cottage had become a top priority since last night's intruder, but her instincts warned that she should proceed with caution. Had her grandmother really paid Wade to stop seeing her? She wanted to dismiss Brie's accusation as nonsense, but the fact that he'd dumped her so abruptly had always niggled.

He said he'd let the rumors of his cheating stand back then so that she would have an easier time moving to Atlanta. In hindsight, maybe she'd accepted that explanation a little too easily. If he really was still keeping things from her, then Brie's claim was a good reminder that she needed to take things slow. Easier said than done, though, since he'd occupied her thoughts so thoroughly these past two days. She wanted to brush off the attraction as a lingering memory of first love, but she needed to be honest with herself. She would have been drawn to Wade Easton had she met him ten years ago or two days ago.

It was still early, but already sunlight blazed across the surface of the lake. The movement of light on water had a calming effect and Abby took her time before calling Wade back. She told him about the break-in and the second warning note, and when she finished, he said simply, "I'm coming over."

She put him off. "No, don't. I have to leave for work soon. We'll meet up later and I'll bring the note. Hopefully, I can get handwriting samples at the office. That is, if you're still willing to take them to your analyst."

"Bring both notes," he said. "And be careful how you go about getting those samples. The situation is starting to heat up. I have some things to tell you, too."

She gripped the phone in alarm. "What things? What's happened?"

"I'd rather we talk in person. Text me a time and place. I'll make sure I'm available."

"Wade—"

"Text me. I'll tell you everything when I see you. And Abby? Be careful."

She had no choice but to leave it at that. A little while later, she stood on the veranda of her mother's house and knocked for a second time to try and rouse her stepfather. When he still didn't answer, she thought about calling Lydia. Maybe he'd had a setback and wasn't well enough to answer the door. Or worse, he might even be back in the hospital.

Standing on tiptoes, she felt along the top of the door frame until her fingers closed around the spare key. Something else had occurred to her while she'd waited for him to answer. If no one was home, this might be the perfect opportunity to search for handwritten notes or letters and anything else that might be incriminating.

She unlocked the door and stuck her head inside. "Hello? Anybody home? It's Abby." She stepped into the foyer and glanced upstairs. "James? Are you awake? I'm here to pick up the paperwork for the Moon Bay Property."

Closing the door softly, she stood for a moment listening to the silence. "Lydia? James? Hello?"

A manila envelope lay on the console table beside her mother's photograph. She hurried over to check the contents. Rather than a scrawled name on the face, Lydia had taken the time to type and print a label. So much for a handwriting sample.

Abby picked up the envelope to scan the contents, but just then a floorboard creaked somewhere above her. Lifting her gaze to the ceiling, she listened intently. Someone was moving down the hall toward the stairs. In a matter of seconds, whoever was up there would be on the landing staring down at her. Common sense told her it was James. She'd called out loudly enough to wake him if he'd been asleep. Maybe he'd forgotten to set the alarm or maybe he'd been in the shower when she first arrived. Whatever the case, Abby had no wish to be caught lurking in the foyer. How would he feel about her using the spare key to let herself in?

She didn't try to analyze her trepidation, but instead, she left the envelope on the table and slipped into the coat closet at the bottom of the stairwell. Her mother had used the narrow space to store seasonal clothing that was rarely used and often forgotten. Stifling a sneeze, Abby pressed herself into the cramped space and tried to ignore the faint scent of lavender sachet that tickled her nostrils.

A few seconds later, she heard someone whistling as they bounded down the stairs. Peering through a crack in the door, she watched as her stepfather paused in the foyer to check himself out in the mirror that hung over the console table.

Gone was the five-o'clock shadow and mussed hair from the day before. In the place of a man recuperating from a serious heart attack was someone who had taken care with his appearance. He continued to whistle as he straightened his collar. Then he smiled at his reflection before he picked up her mother's photo and kissed the image.

Abby stood motionless, heart pounding as she watched him. She tried not to make a sound—the last thing she wanted was to be caught hiding in the coat closet—but his actions disturbed her on so many levels. First of all, she was amazed by his apparent vigor. Observing him now, she could easily imagine he'd had enough strength to drive to Atlanta and throw a rock through her grandmother's window. Or to let himself into the cottage while she slept.

She clamped her lips together as she studied his reflection in the mirror. It was like looking at the image of a stranger. A tall, handsome stranger who looked a good ten years younger than the man who'd sipped lemonade on the veranda less than twenty-four hours ago.

He returned the photograph to the table and then moved from the foyer into the living room, finally disappearing through the cased opening into the dining room and the kitchen beyond. All the while, he continued to whistle as if he didn't have a care in the world.

Abby left her hiding place and slipped across the foyer to exit through the front door, easing it closed behind her. Then she stood on the veranda and took a few deep breaths before she rang the bell.

When James drew back the door, his demeanor instantly shifted. The change was subtle. A furrowed brow. A slight droop to his shoulders. Gone was the vitality she'd witnessed only a few minutes ago. Or was the transformation only her imagination?

"Abby!" He looked past her to the street. "I hope you haven't been waiting long. Sometimes I don't hear the bell if I'm out in the kitchen listening to music."

"I just got here," she fibbed.

He opened the door wider and stepped back. "Would you like to come in? Lydia left some time ago. I was just putting on the coffee. Decaf for me these days, but I'm happy to make a second pot."

"That's a kind offer but I can't stay." Abby tried to act normal, but she couldn't help noting the flicker of puzzlement in his eyes and a slight twitch at the corner of his lips. Maybe he wasn't as composed as he seemed, she thought. "I just came by to pick up the paperwork she left for me."

"Oh, right. For the Moon Bay property. Should be around here somewhere." His gaze lit on the envelope. "Ah, here it is. Let me check…yes, the key is inside." He handed the package to Abby with a flourish. "Are you sure you don't have time for coffee?"

"Thanks, but I should get going. I'm still reading through some of the financial reports Lydia sent over. It'll take me a couple of days to get up to speed."

"I see. Well, my only advice about your meeting with the general contractor is to document everything with notes and photographs. And if you have questions, don't hesitate to call."

"I will."

She turned to leave but he stopped her with a tentative query. "Is everything okay?"

She managed a smile. "Yes, of course. Why?"

"You seem different this morning. Subdued. Are you sure Lydia didn't say something to upset you yesterday while the two of you were alone in the house?"

"We had a very brief conversation," Abby said. "It was nothing. I've already forgotten it."

He didn't look convinced. "I'm well aware of how abrasive she can be. She never warmed up to Eva and I'm afraid she often took her resentment out on you."

"That was in the past. You were right yesterday," Abby said. "Life is too short for bitterness and regrets."

"A word to the wise?"

"Of course."

"Don't let her bully you. She's accustomed to doing things her way so you may have to push back now and then. She'll resist but she'll also respect you for standing up to her."

"I'll remember that."

They said their goodbyes and Abby hurried down the walkway to the street, glancing back once to see if her stepfather watched from the veranda. He didn't. The door to the house was closed and she saw no sign of him at any of the windows. She still didn't know why that earlier glimpse of him at the mirror had left her so unsettled. She already knew that he was on the mend. The doctors were so pleased with his progress he'd been released from the hospital in record time. That he now felt well enough to care about his appearance was a good thing.

She tried to shake off the lingering doubts as she headed out to the street only to halt in her tracks when she saw who waited for her.

BRETT FORTIER LEANED against her car, arms folded, feet crossed, a casual stance that belied everything that had gone down last night on the lake. Despite the sunglasses and the passage of time, he didn't appear to have changed much since high school. A little harder around the edges perhaps, but the smile he flashed was the same lopsided grin that seemed to suggest he knew her deepest, darkest secrets.

He was dressed to blend in with the lake crowd—board shorts, T-shirt and flip-flops— but Abby had a feeling there was nothing spontaneous about his attire or his visit. She hovered on the sidewalk, unsure if she actually wanted to approach him. His reputation preceded him and then some. A part of her wanted to turn and head back to the house while another part—the curious part—stood on the sidewalk staring back at him.

When she was directly across the street from the car, he called over to her. "Heard a rumor you were back in town so I decided to come see for myself."

She crossed the street slowly. "You did more than hear I was back. You were at my house last night. And now here you are again. Should I be worried?"

"Worried? About me?" He chuckled. "I happened to be passing by, saw your car and decided to stop. A complete coincidence, I assure you."

"Right." She drew out the syllable as she gave him a cool appraisal.

"You've gotten cynical." He dipped his head and observed her over the rim of his sunglasses. "You wear it well."

She ignored the comment and kept a safe distance between them. "What were you doing lurking in the bushes outside the cottage last night?"

He grinned in the disarming way he had that made people forget not to trust him. "Lurking is such a loaded word, especially when there's an innocent explanation. I was waiting for my sister."

"How did you know she was there? Did she tell you she was coming to see me?" Abby didn't wait for his answer. "Brie said she hadn't seen you in days and yet there you were waiting for her in my driveway."

He sighed. "Why do I get the feeling this is some kind of interrogation?"

"You would know about interrogations," Abby shot back.

He mocked her with an exaggerated frown. "That hurt."

"But it's true, isn't it?" She placed her hand on the warm car fender. "Brie's visit was extremely odd. I'd never seen her like that. She was tense, secretive. At times even combative. Her attitude only makes sense if you filled her head with nonsense and then sent her to pump me for information."

He feigned innocence. "No one sends my sister anywhere she doesn't want to go. Besides, why would she need a reason to come and see you? You're still her best friend, aren't you?"

"We're friends," Abby said. "But her loyalty will always lie with you."

The teasing faded as he straightened. "Just as yours seems to always lie with Wade Easton."

His tone sent a shiver down her spine. "Why are you here, Brett? What do you want?"

He shrugged. "I just wanted to see you. We used to be friends, too, back in the day. But sure. I'll admit, it would be helpful to know what Wade's up to."

She gazed back at him without reaction. "What makes you think I know anything?"

"I hear you've been spending an awful lot of time with him lately."

"Who told you that?"

"It's not a secret, is it?"

She started to retort that who she saw and what she did was none of his business. Best thing she could do was send Brett Fortier on his way. He was big time trouble and had been since their high school days. But another part of her was curious to find out what *he* knew. Even as a teenager, he was always on the lake. He had a boat before he could drive a car. Maybe he'd seen something ten years ago. A chance meeting or an overheard conversation that would have meant nothing to him then, but could change everything in the context of her mother's murder.

"I can't speak for Wade, but here's what I think," she said. "You sunk your own boat to hide whatever you brought up with you from the Gulf. Probably drugs, probably stolen. Something spooked you so you had to move the product before you were ready. Then you blew up the boat to cover your tracks. Does that sound about right?"

"I admire your imagination," he said. "You always did live in a fantasy world."

"In the past maybe. But I've been grounded in reality for a long time. I see things—and people—for the way they really are."

"Even Wade Easton?"

"Never mind Wade Easton. Are you denying any of what I just said is true?"

The grin flashed again. "Denying nothing, admitting to nothing."

"Then I think we've exhausted the conversation. If you'll just—" She tried to wave him aside. "Do you mind?"

He took his time moving away from the car. "Where's all this hostility coming from? You were never like this before. Is it Wade's influence or have you really changed that much?"

She turned to face him. "You want to know why I'm hostile? You could have killed someone when you blew up that boat last night. Wade was in the water just minutes before you detonated the explosives. Given your history and the current circumstances, I can't help wondering if he was as much a target as your boat."

"You know what they say. If I'd wanted him dead..." He trailed off as he folded his sunglasses and slipped them in his pocket. His eyes were the same icy blue as his sister's. The color was beautiful, but the glittery hardness was not. "He might not be so lucky next time."

Abby narrowed her gaze. "Is that a threat?"

"Just a friendly piece of advice. For his own good—and yours—he needs to lay low for a few days. I'll withdraw my insurance claim if it'll get him off my back. Forget about the explosion and what may or may not have been onboard my boat. Nothing can be proven, anyway. Convince him to walk away before someone gets hurt."

"Wade doesn't walk away."

"He will if you persuade him to. He'll listen to you."

"Since when?"

His gaze dropped almost imperceptibly as he cocked his head. "You really don't give yourself enough credit."

"And you seem intent on giving me too much."

He checked the street behind her. "Maybe you'll be more inclined to see things my way if I tell you what I know."

"I very much doubt it."

He paused, eyes still glittering. "I know what was found at the bottom of the lake."

Her heart started to knock. "What are you talking about?"

"You know exactly what I'm talking about." His tone shifted. "There was a big police presence on the lake early Saturday morning near the old bridge ruins. They brought in divers and at least one salvage boat. If someone got curious about all the excitement, they might have asked around. It's possible they did a little more than ask."

"By *they*, I assume you mean you." Even as Abby told herself not to fall for his ploy, she found herself asking, "What is it you think you know?"

"Ten years ago, your mother planned to leave town with her lover. For a price, I'll tell you the name of her mystery man."

Abby stared at him in shock. Was he telling the truth?

"Do we have a deal?" he prompted.

"How can I agree to something I can't deliver," she said in frustration. "Contrary to what you seem to think, I don't have any pull with Wade Easton. Not anymore. I'm not sure I ever did. I can ask him to back off, but if he's anything like he used to be, he'll just dig his heels in that much deeper."

"In that case, I guess we really don't have anything more to discuss." He started to walk away but she stopped him.

"Wait. You can't just drop a bombshell like that and leave me hanging. If you have information regarding my mother, then please, just tell me what you know."

"Even if it circles back to Wade Easton? He's not the man you think he is, Abby."

"How do you know what I think?"

He pinned her with a penetrating stare. "You really want to know what happened ten years ago?"

"Of course, I do. But I want to talk about my mother's disappearance, not Wade Easton."

"What if I told you they're connected?"

She tried to ignore the tug of fear that threatened her composure. "I'd say you're lying."

"But I'm not and I think a part of you already suspects that he hasn't been honest with you." He leaned in. "Wade has always been real good at keeping secrets."

Like accepting money from her grandmother to break up with her? She moistened her suddenly dry lips. "What secrets?"

His gaze darted past her to the house. "This isn't the place for a heavy discussion. We've been standing out in the open for too long."

"Are you worried about being a target?"

"Always," he said with a careless shrug. "But besides that, your stepfather has been watching you like a hawk ever since you left the house."

Abby turned, lifting her gaze to the upstairs window where James stared down at them. She felt a sudden chill though she couldn't say why exactly. Maybe her disquiet had something to do with his earlier behavior or maybe it was because the man with whom she stood talking to had nearly killed Wade the night before and had all but confessed to blowing up his own boat. It was an unnerving moment to stay the least. She wasn't sure who she could trust anymore. Certainly not Brett Fortier. But even knowing what she knew about Brie's brother, his provocation worked. She wasn't about to walk away yet.

"Where do you suggest we talk?" she asked.

"I know a place. Quiet but not too remote. Or, if you prefer, you pick the spot."

"There's a small cafe on Front Street that overlooks the lake. We can get coffee and sit out under the trees." Private but within shouting distance of help if she needed it.

He grinned as if reading her mind. "My car or yours?"

"Both. I'll meet you there."

He winked. "Lead the way."

He opened her car door and waited for her to climb inside. Abby tracked him from the rearview mirror. He headed toward a luxury SUV parked at the curb. Black, heavily tinted windows. Expensive. A vehicle that made a statement. What that statement was, she wasn't quite sure. In the split second before she started the engine, she thought, *Am I really doing this?* She could only imagine what her stepfather must think. Or what Wade would say. However, this was her decision.

She glanced at the upstairs window again, but James was nowhere to be seen.

ABBY DROVE THROUGH TOWN, still with one eye on the rearview mirror. Brett was still back there. Not exactly riding her bumper, but close enough to make her anxious. The thought crossed her mind more than once that she should just lose him. Make a quick turn and put some distance between them. Then she shrugged off her foreboding with a reminder that if he'd wanted to hurt her, he could have easily done so the night before. He had an agenda. Of that she felt certain. But they were meeting in a public place in broad daylight. What would be the harm in hearing what he had to say? Maybe he knew something about her mother and maybe he didn't. Maybe he knew something about Wade and maybe he didn't. Either way, she wasn't about to turn back now.

The Oleander Café was one of several shops and restaurants situated along a narrow one-way street bordering a wooded park that swooped down toward the lake. A few blocks to the south, the new bridge—a metal monstrosity of girders and cables—loomed over the low-rise skyline. Traffic was heavy on the main thoroughfares, and she could see a steady stream of boats puttering to and from the marina. Good. She'd counted on having plenty of people around.

She quickly found a parking space, but Brett had to circle a few times to locate a spot wide enough to accommodate the SUV. Abby didn't wait for him. She went inside and ordered two black coffees, then carried both drinks outside. When he finally caught up with her, she handed him a cup. He accepted with a cheery thanks and then followed her down the wooded embankment toward the picnic tables that overlooked the water.

Only a handful of people were seated at the scattered tables. She indicated her choice with a wave of her coffee cup.

Once they were settled, he said, "Nice spot. I'm surprised your mother's company hasn't bulldozed this block to build condos." When she didn't respond, he folded his arms on the table and leaned in. "Maybe you could build them yourself if you manage to wrest control of the business from the evil Lydia."

Did he really expect her to talk business after the shock he'd created earlier? "I'm only here to help out until my stepfather is back on his feet. But I have a feeling you already know that."

"You still live in Atlanta?"

She frowned. "What is the point of these questions?"

He shrugged. "No point. Just catching up. There was a time when you and I were a bit more than friendly."

Her reply was blunt. "You remember things differently than I do."

He grinned. "The way *I* remember it, we were a good match until Wade came along."

"Now who's living in a fantasy world?" She lifted her chin. "I do remember how much you liked to cause trouble. Brie had to bail you out of one scrape after another. I have a feeling nothing much has changed since then."

"You might be surprised."

"I doubt it." She gazed across the lake at the marina wondering from which slot his boat had been stolen. Allegedly stolen. "Can we just get on with this? You made a provocative statement earlier about Wade and my mother's disappearance. I'm still waiting to see if you can follow through on what I consider an outrageous claim."

He pried off the plastic lid to sip his coffee

from the cup. "Did you know I used to work for your mother?"

Abby nodded. "I have a vague recollection. She employed a lot of high school kids during the summer. What was your job?"

"You name it, I did it. I started out part-time and then she gradually increased my workload until I was putting in ten to twelve hours a day. I did everything from filing paperwork at the courthouse to ferrying clients up and down the lake in one of the company's boats."

"What kind of clients?"

"Investors, prospective buyers and the like. She had a lot of property she was looking to unload. I'd heard rumors about a condo project, and I got curious about some of the big money she was courting from the Gulf Coast. I decided to pay attention to who came and went from her rentals. I figured it wouldn't hurt to make a few contacts. Maybe some of those high rollers could be useful to me in the future. But the more I saw, the more I saw. If you get my drift."

"I'm not sure that I do."

"Put it this way. I started to observe not only her business associates, but also Eva herself. Where she went and who she spent time with."

"In other words, you spied on her."

"If you want to be blunt. That's how I found out she was having an affair. I saw them together.

And I'd be willing to bet she met this person on the bridge the night she supposedly left town."

Abby didn't want to appear too eager, but she couldn't help herself. "Who was he? Give me a name."

Brett let the mystery play out for a moment. "Are you sure you want to know? There's no going back once you find out his identity."

Her heart pounded even harder. "Just tell me."

His smile turned smug. "Sam Easton. The chief of police. Your boyfriend's father. *That* Sam Easton."

Abby sucked in a sharp breath. "I don't believe you."

He lifted his coffee cup. She couldn't help noticing that his hand was steady. "You can believe me or not. I'm telling you what I know to be a fact."

"How can you be so sure?"

"I told you. I saw them together."

"Where?"

"They met several afternoons a week in one of her rental houses."

Abby sat quietly for a moment. "Did anyone else know?"

"Besides Wade, you mean?"

Her gaze shot back to Brett. "What makes you think he knew?"

"I've always been good at reading people. I

let a few things slip and watched his expression. He didn't have much of a poker face back then."

"If he knew, he would have told me," Abby said without much conviction.

"You understand why he didn't, right? He was afraid his old man had something to do with your mother's disappearance."

"I don't believe that."

"Poor Abby, All these years, Wade Easton has been protecting his family at the expense of yours."

Chapter Twelve

By midafternoon, Wade was headed back out to the lake. Detective Benson had called to inform him the equipment was on-site, and the salvage operation would soon be underway. With any luck, the car would be lifted and transported to a protected lot and the remains to the morgue within the hour.

He tried to call Abby, but she didn't answer, so he left a voicemail and then a text message. He hated to deliver the news in such an impersonal manner, and a part of him wondered if he should have told her at all. Her mother's car swinging over the water was a sight she wouldn't easily forget. If he could have spared her that memory, he would have, but he'd kept too many things from her as it was.

By the time he arrived on the scene, the divers were all geared up and waiting in a boat while a few uniformed officers milled about on the bank. The crane operator climbed into the cab, and after a few false starts, extended the boom out over the water and lowered the jib. The divers rolled backward off the side of the boat and went down to secure the hooks to the vehicle.

Detective Benson stood at the edge of the water to observe the operation. Wade didn't call out to him or try to approach. Instead, he took a position at the top of the embankment, where he hoped to keep a low profile.

He'd been waiting in the shade for only a few minutes when a shout from one of the crew members drew his gaze back down to the bank. The hustle of activity around the equipment caught his attention first. Something had obviously malfunctioned. As he scanned the area, he spotted a solitary figure standing apart from the other spectators. Recognition jolted him. He studied his dad's profile for a moment before he scrambled down the embankment to join him.

Sam Easton appeared deep in contemplation as he stared out at the dive boat. When Wade touched his shoulder, he visibly jumped before he turned.

Wade took a step back. "Sorry. I didn't mean to startle you."

"Then don't sneak up on me," his dad grumbled.

"I wasn't trying to sneak up on you. I thought you heard me coming."

"Well, I didn't. Lost in thought, I guess." He turned back to the water.

Yes, Wade thought. There was a lot to consider. He wondered what was going through his dad's head at that moment. A woman he'd had an affair with had been murdered, her body hidden beneath the lake for a decade. He claimed the relationship had been over by the time Eva left town, yet here he was.

"What's going on?" Wade asked.

"Cable snapped. That'll cause a delay."

"How long do you think?"

His dad shrugged. "Minutes, hours, a day. Depends on whether they can repair it on-site."

"That's not good," Wade said. "I don't like the idea of that car being underwater for another night."

His dad shot him a glance. "You think someone might try to destroy evidence?"

"That thought crossed my mind." Wade paused. "What are you doing out here, anyway? How did you know they were bringing the car up today?"

"Roy Benson called. He thought I'd want to be here."

"Why?"

The question seemed to annoy him. He sounded impatient when he tried to explain his rationale. "I already told you. The car went over the bridge while I was still the chief. Someone was apparently murdered on my watch. I feel responsible."

"Is that the only reason you're here?"

His dad's mouth tightened in anger, but he didn't respond.

"Well, is it?" Wade pressed.

Despite his dad's anger, he seemed to measure his words carefully. "I'm not going to let you goad me into saying something we both might later regret. You've got a problem with what happened in the past. I get it. But I can't go back and change what I did, and I'm not going to keep apologizing for it. Where that leaves us is up to you."

Wade's own temper flared, but he tamped it back down. The past couldn't be changed no matter what either of them said. Provoking his dad was at best a petty satisfaction.

"I'm sorry. I was out of line."

He sighed. "You don't owe me an apology. I let you down. I let your mother down. You've a right to your resentment. But I'd like to set all that aside for a moment and talk about what happened out here on the lake last night. Detective Benson said someone set charges beneath the surface and blew up a boat. I assume that's why you're worried about sabotage, but I'm more concerned about your safety. He said you were in the water just minutes before the explosion. You could have been badly injured or killed."

Wade tried to downplay the close call. "But I wasn't."

His dad frowned. "You don't seem to be taking this seriously. I warned you about the kind of people that would come looking for that boat."

"And I told you I know how to take care of myself. Besides, I'm reasonably certain Brett Fortier blew up his own boat."

"Is that supposed to make me feel better? Don't underestimate him," his dad warned.

"I don't underestimate anyone when enough money is involved."

"Good." He stared at the activity on the water in silent contemplation for a moment. "Benson said Abby Dallas was with you last night. Are you sure you want to start that up again?"

Wade's temper stirred yet again as he scowled in response. "Start what up again?"

"You know damn well what I mean. You were way too serious about that girl in high school. Teenagers do foolish things when their hormones are raging."

"Adults too," Wade muttered.

His dad ignored the insinuation. "Have you ever stopped to consider who stood to benefit the most from Eva's death?"

Wade didn't like where the conversation appeared to be heading. "What are you getting at, Dad?"

"Abby was her mother's sole heir. She stands to inherit Eva's estate once the dust settles."

"How do you know anything about Eva McRae's will?"

"She told me."

Wade wanted to believe the conversation was nothing more than idle speculation, but something seemed to be brewing beneath the surface. A subtle machination that he hadn't expected from his dad. He wanted to blurt out an irate retort, but instead he took his time to reply. "You're surely not suggesting Abby had anything to do with her mother's death."

"It's not as far-fetched as you make it out to be."

"Yes, it is. Think about what you're saying. A seventeen-year-old with no history of violence lured her mother to the lake, pushed her car off the bridge and then waited ten years for someone to discover the wreckage so that she could collect an inheritance."

"Not someone. You."

Wade felt baffled. He stared at his dad in disbelief. "Are you implying I had something to do with Eva's death?"

"No, of course not. But you told me yesterday to look at the situation through the eyes of an outsider. You should do the same. Don't think for a minute Detective Benson isn't already compiling a list of suspects. Be careful how you deal with him," his dad advised. "And make damn sure you don't let yourself become a patsy."

"A patsy?"

"Remember what you said earlier. Never underestimate anyone when enough money is involved."

Wade let the implication sink in for a moment. "You couldn't be more wrong about Abby. But I'll return the favor and give you the same advice. Be careful how you deal with Detective Benson. He has a lot of questions about the way you handled Eva's disappearance."

His dad frowned. "Why would he have questions? We had no reason to suspect foul play at the time. How could we? Everyone assumed she left town of her own accord."

"He thinks you accepted that story a little too easily."

There was a note of something that might have been fear in his dad's voice. "He said that?"

Wade nodded. "He also said you kept a file on Eva going back years. But you told me you never suspected she was involved in anything illegal."

"I never had anything concrete to go on," he said. "Just a few rumors that cropped up now and then. It was my job to check them out. Nothing ever came of them. As far as I know, she was a straight arrow when it came to her business."

"Did you plan on leaving town with her?"

A shout from the dive boat caught his dad's attention. He watched the commotion without answering.

"Dad?"

"I loved your mother. I was never going to leave her for another woman."

That didn't precisely answer his question, but Wade didn't press. Maybe he was afraid of the answer.

"You were right about Benson," he said. "He's a dog with a bone. The longer and deeper he digs, the more likely Mom is to find out about the affair. If she doesn't already know."

"She doesn't."

"How can you be so sure? You didn't think I knew, either."

"I'm telling you, she doesn't know," his dad insisted.

Wade lowered his voice. "Then why did she come out here last night? To this very spot? Why was she staring at the water in the exact place where the car went over the bridge?"

His dad looked taken aback. "What are you talking about? She never left the house last night."

"She did. I saw her."

His dad's tone turned icy. "I don't know what you think you saw, but I'm telling you your mother was in her studio all night."

"Dad, I saw her."

"Let it go. Do you hear me? *Let it go.*"

His rigid denial shook Wade. He had the resolved demeanor of a man trying to hide something. Or protect someone.

Before Wade could react, something drew his

focus back up the embankment to the place where he'd seen his mother the night before. For a moment, he thought she might have returned, but then he realized the person who stood staring down at him was Abby.

Their gazes held for the longest moment before she turned and walked away. By the time Wade climbed to the top of the embankment, she was nowhere to be found.

Chapter Thirteen

Wade was waiting for Abby on the dock steps when she got home late that afternoon. He sat with his arms folded over his knees watching a small sailboat glide across the cove. Hovering at the top of the stairs, Abby stared down at him for the longest time. She didn't want to believe him capable of accepting money to break up with her, let alone withholding information about her mother's death, but neither could she dismiss the claims out of hand. She didn't really know him anymore. Maybe she never had, she thought morosely as she started down the stairs.

He turned at the sound of her footsteps. "There you are."

"I hope you haven't been waiting too long. There's so much to catch up on at the office. More files and records than I'll ever be able to wade through. Time got away from me."

"No problem. I never get tired of this view." He moved over so she could sit beside him and then handed her a set of keys. "You left earlier before I had a chance to give you these."

"Thank you for taking care of the locks," she said. "I'll sleep a lot better tonight."

"So will I."

She toyed with the keys for a moment. "Were they able to lift the car?" She sounded stilted and reluctant even to her ears.

He gave her a sidelong glance, as if trying to figure out her mood. "Yes. The Wraith is in a locked compound at the police station. Everything is where it's supposed to be."

Meaning the remains had been transported to the morgue. Abby gave a brief nod as she hugged her knees to her chest. "I'm sorry I left so abruptly. Turns out, the salvage operation was a lot more emotional than I thought it would be."

His gaze was still on her. "You don't need to apologize for anything. I'm the one who owes you an apology."

"For what?"

"There's something I need to tell you about that last summer." His voice turned solemn, remorseful. "I should have told you a long time ago. Now I don't even know where to start."

She braced herself for his confession. "I think I know what you're about to say. My mother had an affair with your father. And you kept it from me."

He stared back at her in astonishment. "How long have you known?"

"Brett Fortier told me this morning."

His expression darkened. "Brett Fortier? How did that happen?"

"He tracked me down at my stepfather's house. He wanted to make a deal."

Wade's voice turned cynical. "Oh, I can't wait to hear about this," he muttered. "What kind of deal?"

"He would tell me what he knew about my mother's disappearance if I persuaded you to drop your investigation. He said you needed to lay low for a few days."

"At least he's consistent. He told me the same thing last night."

Now she was the one taken aback. "You saw Brett last night? Where?"

"At the bridge ruins." He shifted his gaze to the sailboat, lifting his hand briefly when the young sailors waved at them. "After I met with Detective Benson, I stayed in the area to keep an eye out."

"Why didn't you tell me? I would have gone with you."

"There was no need for both of us to stand guard."

"I disagree. We're supposed to be in this to-gether." She studied his profile. "So Brett was at the ruins?"

"Yes, but we didn't meet face-to-face. Well, not exactly face-to-face." He massaged the back of his head. "He had a few tricks up his sleeve to get my attention."

"What kind of tricks?" she asked in alarm.

"We'll get into that later. The intent of the interaction was to warn me to back off. He said none of it would matter in a few days, anyway."

"What do you think he meant?"

"I'm guessing it had something to do with whatever he salvaged from the boat."

"Drugs?"

"I'd bet money on it. That's why he expects everything to be resolved soon. He's probably found a buyer. A quick payday will allow him to disappear without the insurance settlement."

"You still think someone's after him?"

He glanced her way. "Would that surprise you?"

"No. In fact, it would explain why he didn't want to be out in the open. He said he always worries about being a target."

"Even more reason to steer clear of him," Wade said. "A hunted man on a time line is a dangerous man. He'll consider anyone who gets in his way a threat. Last night, we both witnessed how far he's willing to go to cover his tracks."

"I'm well aware of the danger," Abby said. "But I didn't seek him out. He came to me. And I'm glad he did. He told me something about my mother that I needed to know. He said the reason you kept it from me was because you were protecting your dad." She paused on a shiver. "Is that true?"

"He got in your head," Wade said. "He's good at that."

"You didn't answer my question."

He continued to evade. "Is that the reason you left the salvage area earlier without speaking to me earlier? You weren't just emotional about the operation. Seeing me with my dad confirmed what Brett had told you earlier."

She started to deny his charge, then shrugged. "Okay. He did plant doubts. But that doesn't make what he said any less true. You kept something important from me, Wade. Even after I hired you to help me investigate my mother's murder, you withheld vital information. I'm only human. A part of me has to wonder if you agreed to take the case so that you'd have control of the evidence."

He didn't look pleased with her assessment. "I took the case because I wanted to help you find the truth. Brett is very convincing. It's why he's such a good con man. But not everything he told you is true. I wasn't protecting my dad," he said. "I was protecting my mother."

"Why?"

He squinted at the water. "That was the summer her doctor diagnosed her with clinical depression. The medication she was given didn't help much back then. Some days she could barely muster the will to get out of bed. She was sad, lonely, distant. She seemed to be wasting away before our eyes, and my dad and I were powerless to help her. There were times during the worst of it when I was afraid to go home. Afraid of what I might find when I opened the door."

Abby swallowed back a sudden lump. "I didn't know."

"When I saw them together—my dad and your mother—all I could think was how the affair would hurt my mother. She was already in so much pain. I wanted to tell you, but I couldn't take the chance it would somehow get back to her."

"I wouldn't have told anyone."

His smile was sad. "Not on purpose, but you might have let something slip. I wasn't willing to take that chance. For my mother's sake, I couldn't. Then Eva left, and I thought keeping that secret from you would get easier, but it didn't. Her disappearance just made me worry that I might come home one day to find that my dad had packed his bags and left, too. How would I take care of my mother on my own?"

"That's a heavy burden for a seventeen-year-old," she said in a soft voice.

He dismissed her acknowledgment. "It was selfish, actually. Worrying about how everything would affect me. I wasn't mature enough to consider all the angles. The only way I knew to help my mom was to keep my mouth shut."

"You weren't selfish," she said almost fiercely. "Your protectiveness is admirable. Noble, even."

"I wasn't noble. I was scared. And I hurt you because of it. When Brie started the rumor that I'd been with someone else, I didn't deny it because in some ways, it was easier to let you hate me."

She stared at him for the longest moment. "What makes you think Brie started the rumor?"

"I was told by a friend it came from her. Made sense. She and I never got along. It was no secret how much she disliked me." He glanced her way. "I think she wanted you to be with Brett."

Abby thought back to her conversation with Brie the night before. "I don't think Brett had anything to do with it. I've been going back over some of the conversations Brie and I had over the years. Certain things she let slip from time to time. I think she was in love with you."

He looked taken aback. "What? No. I never got that vibe from her."

"She hid her emotions well, but it's so clear to me now," Abby said. "It explains so much about her attitude since you've been back. She told me that my grandmother paid you to break up with me."

"That never happened."

"I know. But after Brett told me about the affair, you can see why I jumped to conclusions. You were right. I let both of them get in my head.

That is why I avoided you at the lake earlier. That's why I didn't return your calls and texts. I needed time to sort through their accusations. They played me. They've both done everything they could to discredit you in my eyes, and I let them. I'm sorry."

He reached over and brushed back a strand of hair from her face. "Like I said. You don't owe me an apology. You don't owe me anything. If I'd been straight with you from the start, they wouldn't have been able to manipulate either of us. I'm sorry for my part in all this. I'm deeply sorry for the pain I caused you. I wish I could go back and change things, but I can't. The past is past."

She nodded. "I know."

"It does make you wonder about their motive, though, doesn't it? How do you suppose Brett found out about the affair?"

"He worked for my mother that summer. He started following her around to see if he could make inroads with some of the money people she brought to the lake, and apparently, he saw them together."

"He never told anyone until now?"

She shrugged. "I guess not."

Wade looked skeptical. "That doesn't sound like Brett. It's not like him to pass up an opportunity. Even back then, he was always looking for an angle. If he tried to blackmail your mother, that could explain the large amount of cash she withdrew. It could also explain why he seems hell-bent on pinning her murder on my dad."

"And Brie?"

"She's always covered for him. You know that better than anyone."

"Yes, but to think she's pretended to be my friend when she's known all along what happened to my mother…that's a bitter pill to swallow," Abby said.

"It's speculation at this point."

"I know. But it makes sense."

"We don't know anything yet. Try to keep an open mind."

"Can you?"

He let out a breath. "I'm trying."

In the brief silence that followed, she felt something shift between them. The air had been cleared, leaving an intimacy that was at once comforting and unsettling. They talked for a long time, until the sun dipped below the horizon and twilight settled in with a breeze. The fireflies came out and then the mosquitoes. Abby rose and brushed her hand across his shoulder before she started up the steps. Their gazes connected, and then he rose slowly and came up the steps behind her. She used one of the new keys to let them in through the patio door. Inside, he drew her to him, and they kissed.

When they finally parted, she said in a near whisper, "Is this a mistake?"

He rested his forehead against hers. "Time will tell, I guess. It doesn't feel like a mistake."

"To me, either." She took his hand and led him down the hallway. The bedroom was cool and dim. She sat on the edge of the bed while he went over to the window to glance out.

"It'll be dark soon," he said.

"You like the water by moonlight."

He smiled. "Yes, I do." He came over and sat down beside her. "You seem nervous."

"I guess I am a little."

"There's no need to be." He took her hand and entwined their fingers. "Today was hard. Lots of bad things going on out there." He nodded to the window. "In here, it's just you and me."

She lay back on the bed and he joined her. "Do you know what I find strange? How difficult it's been to adjust my perception. For so many years, I thought my mother abandoned me. It shaped my life in ways I probably still don't understand. I don't trust easily. I don't make friends easily. But the strangest part of all is that her murder doesn't really change anything. Because she actually did plan to leave me."

"Yes, but given the opportunity, she might have had a change of heart." He rolled to his side to gaze at her profile. "Or she might have come back for you."

"I'll never know." She turned to face him. "About that trust thing...before we go any farther, I need to ask you something. Is there anything else you haven't told me?"

His hesitation made her heart skip a beat. Then he brushed his knuckles down the side of her face and said, "There's something you should know about me."

She tried to brace herself. "What is it?"

"I think I'm still in love with you."

ABBY WAS UTTERLY stunned by his confession. She remained speechless for so long that the silence became awkward. "I...never expected that."

"Neither did I, if I'm honest. It's not like I've been pining all these years."

"Thanks."

He smiled. "All I'm saying is that I've lived a full life since I left this place. I've traveled the world and had my fill of adventures. It's been a good life and I've been happy. But Saturday morning, my first sight of you on the terrace hit me like a ton of bricks. It sounds like a bad piece of melodrama, but that's the best way I know to describe how I felt."

"If we're being honest...it hit me like that, too," she admitted. "I've also lived a life. Maybe I wasn't as adventurous as you. Maybe not as happy as you. But I carved out a nice place for myself in Atlanta. Seeing you after so many years has disrupted everything. I never expected to still care. To still want you. I haven't been able to stop thinking about you. I don't know if that's love, but I do know it's something powerful." She rose and started taking off her clothes.

When only her underwear remained, he stood, too, and tugged his shirt over his head. He ran a hand down her arm, drawing a shiver. Then he kissed her as he unsnapped her bra and tossed it aside. They fell back on the bed once more, lips crushed together, hips moving in unison until a shuddering release left them spent, panting and laughing softly in wonder.

Chapter Fourteen

Abby awakened the next morning to the smell of fresh coffee. She drew on her robe and followed the scent out to the kitchen. Wade sat barefoot and shirtless on the terrace with his phone. She poured a cup, retrieved an envelope from her bag and went outside to join him.

He looked up with a smile that quickened her breath. "Good morning. Hope the coffee's not too strong for you."

"I like strong coffee."

He put away his phone and leaned his arms on the table. "How did you sleep last night?"

"Better than I have in a long time." She eyed him over the rim of her cup. "Except for when you kept me up."

He sat back and folded his hands behind his head. "I remember it differently. You were the one who kept me up."

"Let's not quibble over petty details." She took a tentative sip of her coffee. "Wow. That is strong."

"Don't say I didn't warn you. What's in the envelope?"

She handed him the packet. "Handwriting samples from work. Signatures mostly, but I did find handwritten notations on some old work orders. I labeled them so you would know who they belonged to. The warning notes are also inside for comparison."

He removed the contents and thumbed through the pages. "No one saw you take these?"

"I was careful. Lydia is out of town, so that made things a little easier. How long do you think the analysis will take?"

"I'll scan and email this morning. But the analyst will probably want the originals to make an informed decision. I'll have to overnight them, so be prepared to wait at least a couple of days." He spread the pages on the table and scrutinized the signatures.

Abby said anxiously, "What do you think?"

He shrugged. "I'm no expert. Take what I say with a grain of salt. Could be nothing more than the power of suggestion, but I do see a similarity with the notes."

"Show me." She got up and came around the table to stand behind him.

"Compare Lydia's signature on some of the work orders with the warning notes. The loop through the lowercase *a* is similar. See what I mean?"

Abby squinted. "Not really. That seems a common way to write a lowercase *a* to me. And, anyway, now that I think about it, why wouldn't the person who wrote those notes disguise their handwriting?"

"Maybe they were in a hurry." He gathered up the pages and returned them to the envelope. "In any case, we'll see what a real expert has to say." He slid the envelope aside and picked up his coffee. "What else is on the day's agenda?"

"I'm sure Detective Benson has been to see James by now, and he'll have informed Lydia about Mother's murder. She won't be back until late this afternoon, so I should probably stop by and make sure he's okay. At least I won't have to pretend not to know things."

"Just be careful. Remember, no one has been ruled out as a suspect."

"I'll be fine." But she sounded far more confident than she felt. Her stepfather's odd behavior the day before had left her uncomfortable. "Before that, I'm meeting with a general contractor at one of our properties in the Moon Bay neighborhood."

"Moon Bay?" He frowned.

"It's just a few miles north of here."

"I remember the area as being fairly isolated," he said.

"Not anymore. Hardly any place on the lake is isolated these days."

"Moon Bay." He repeated the name, then glanced away as if something had occurred to him.

"What?" she prompted.

"With everything going on, I don't think it's a good idea for you to be alone with a stranger. Give me the address. I'll clear my schedule and meet you there."

She complied, then said, "Why did you get that look on your face when I mentioned Moon Bay?"

"What look?"

"Like you remembered something. What's going on?"

"I've been out there before," he said.

She didn't make the connection at first, but then the significance of the place dawned on her. "Wait. Is that where you saw them together?" She winced. "Now I won't be able to get that picture out of my head."

"It may not even be the same house," he said. "They probably used whatever place was empty at the time."

But the image wouldn't go away, and a little while later when Abby let herself in the front door of the rental, she could almost hear the echoes of their passion . She'd made sure to arrive early so that she could walk the property before the general contractor arrived. Wade wasn't around, either. She thumbed a message to let him know she'd arrived and then put her phone away as she stepped from the foyer into the large family room. A wall of windows provided an amazing view of the lake.

She started forward only to halt with a gasp. For a moment she stood frozen, her gaze pinned to the body on the floor. To Brett Fortier's ashen face. Blood puddled beneath his head. He didn't appear to be breathing.

Heart pounding, she fished for her phone as she hurried across the room to offer assistance even though instinct and the pallor of his skin told her that he was dead. How could anyone survive a wound that produced so much blood?

Her first thought was that he'd been murdered by whoever had come looking for his boat. The killer might still be in the house—

"Put away the phone," a familiar voice said behind her.

She whirled in shock.

Her stepfather gestured with the barrel of his gun. "Put the phone on the floor and back away from the body."

"James?" She stared at him in horror. "What have you done?" she asked in a near whisper.

His features hardened into someone she barely recognized. "Do as I say. The phone. Now!"

She put the phone on the floor and slowly rose. "What are you doing?"

"Isn't it obvious? I'm protecting myself." His

gaze dropped to the body. "He was a drug dealer. Think of how many lives he ruined. I wouldn't waste my time mourning the lies of Brett Fortier if I were you."

"He was a human being!" she cried, still unable to put the pieces together. "How did killing him protect you?"

"Do I really have to spell it out? Anyone who knew Brett Fortier could have predicted his demise years ago. The police will conclude that you walked in on a drug deal gone bad. His buyers panicked and took you both out."

Abby swallowed. He was right. The police would come to the same conclusion she had, but not Wade. He would never buy such an easy explanation. He would keep digging even if it meant putting himself in danger.

Wade. She drew a breath and tried to slow her racing heart. He would be here soon and he had no idea what he would be walking into. She had to stay calm while she searched for a way out. She had to remain alive so that she could warn him. "Wade Easton will never let you get away with this. You know that, don't you?"

He smiled, showing a hint of the old charming James. "I doubt he'll have much credibility once the local authorities realize he and his father have been lying to them for years." He feigned surprise. "Oh, wait. You didn't think I knew about the affair?"

"What affair?"

He gave a low chuckle. "You never were a good liar. Unlike your mother." He took a step into the room. "Oh, I knew all right. She never bothered to hide it. The covert phone calls in the middle of the night. The new hairstyle, the new underwear. All the working late excuses. And to think, I left my first wife for that...woman. One could almost appreciate the irony."

"That was a long time ago," Abby said. "Surely, you're not still holding a grudge. You can't blame me for what happened."

"Blame you? No. I've always been fond of you."

"Then what do you want?" she asked in desperation. "Money? The company? You don't have to do this. We can make a deal."

"A deal that will expire as soon as I let you walk out that door." His shook his head. "Give me more credit than that. I've poured my life into that company, *your* company, and for what? So that you can waltz in and take what should rightfully be mine?"

"That was never my intention," Abby said. "I don't want the company. I never wanted it."

"Maybe not now, but you would eventually. Big things are in the works. I've put together the kind of deals that Eva could only dream about. All that money. You wouldn't be able to resist."

Abby shifted her position imperceptibly, putting her weight on her back foot so that she could try and make a run for it if and when the opportunity arose. "What did Brett have to do with any of this?"

"His arrival in town was serendipitous. When I heard about his stolen boat, I figured he was up to his neck in something dangerous. Drugs, most likely. We'd crossed paths before, he and I. In fact, we had an arrangement. I'd let him hole up in a rental now and then when he needed a place to lay low."

"Why would you do that?"

Another quick smile. "In addition to dealing drugs, Brett dabbled in blackmail."

"What did he have on you?"

"Can't you guess?"

Abby's hands tightened into fists at her sides. "He saw you on the bridge the night my mother was murdered."

"Now are you starting to put it all together?"

A wave of red-hot hanger washed over her. "You're a monster. You couldn't just kill her outright. You wanted to watch her suffer."

"You don't think she deserved it?"

"No one deserves what you did to her. All these years, you let everyone believe she ran off with another man."

He waved the gun in her direction. "You want the cold, hard truth about that night? Your mother was a heartless bitch. She would have left her only child without a backward glance if not for Sam Easton's conscience. He got cold feet at the last minute. He called it off, but she couldn't accept his rejection."

"How do you know that?"

"Because I heard her on the phone. She pleaded with him to meet her at the bridge, to give her one last chance. That must have killed her, having to beg for a man's affection." He smirked.

"So you went instead," Abby said. "And Brett saw what you did."

"We came to an agreement that worked out well over the years, but people like him always get greedy. They always start clawing for more. I knew it was only a matter of time before I'd have to find a permanent solution to his blackmail. It may sound strange, but my heart attack turned out to be fortuitous. I had days and days in the hospital to plan. All I had to do was get you back here. Then make it look as though you were simply in the wrong place at the wrong time."

"But you didn't count on Mother's body being found, did you?"

"An interesting confluence of events," he said. "But it doesn't change anything. With you out of the way, the business is mine."

"What about Lydia?"

"What about her?"

Abby inched toward the patio door. "Does she know about your plan?"

"She's a wonderful daughter, but a little thick sometimes. I could never trust her with something this important. Why do you think I arranged for her to be out of town? It'll be over by the time she returns."

"She may not be as clueless as you think," Abby said. "She's been trying to warn me."

He scoffed at the notion of his daughter's betrayal. "Don't be ridiculous. She doesn't know anything."

"Maybe she does. Maybe she knows everything. What if she decides the business should be hers? You've got a bad heart. It wouldn't take much—"

"Stop," he said. "I see what you're trying to do. Take another step toward the door and I'll drop you where you stand."

"Why haven't you already pulled the trigger?" Abby taunted. "Why take the time to tell me all about your plan? Maybe you want me to appreciate how clever you are. Or maybe it's proving harder than you thought it would be."

"What are you talking about?"

"Killing me in cold blood. You can't quite bring yourself to do it, can you? That's why it's taking so long."

She worried that she'd goaded him too far, but then her ringtone sounded, and they both jumped. Her gaze shot to the phone. "That'll be Wade. He's on his way here. He may be outside already.

If you shoot me now, he'll hear the gunshots. You won't be able to get away from him."

James looked momentarily panicked. His gaze darted around the room before coming back to her. "You're lying."

"I'm not. He didn't want me to come out here alone. He said he would meet me here. He'll be at the door any minute."

"You better hope that's not true."

He took a step back into the foyer so that he could glance out the window. Abby reacted instinctively. She lunged for the patio door, fumbling with the lock and then ducking as a shot rang out. Then she was out the door and flying down the dock steps. She screamed and waved her arms at a passing boat. The passengers waved back and were gone by the time James came after her.

Desperate now, he fired from the top of the steps. She dove off the dock and swam to the bottom, holding her breath until her lungs forced her to surface. Keeping to the side of the dock, she pressed up against the bumpers as she eased through the water to the bank.

James stood at the end of the platform gazing down into the water where she'd gone in. For a moment, Abby considered hoisting herself on the dock and catching him by surprise. She had to make a move soon. She couldn't hide in the water forever.

As she vacillated, she saw movement out of the corner of her eye. Before she had time to catch her breath, Wade rushed down the steps and flew past her at a dead run. James whirled at the sound of his footsteps. He fired as Wade slammed into him. The momentum toppled them into the lake.

Abby scrambled up on the dock and ran to the end, dropping to her knees as she tried to peer through the murk. She didn't know whether Wade had been hit or not. They were underwater for what seemed an eternity. Then James bobbled to the surface. She stared at him in horror, bracing herself until she realized something was wrong with him. Wade came up then, grabbed James and heaved him onto the platform.

"We need a phone," he said on a breath. "I think he's having a heart attack."

For a moment, Abby just stood staring down at her stepfather as the image of another struggle played out in her head. James handcuffing her mother to the steering wheel and then watching from the bridge as the car sank to the bottom.

"Abby, move!"

She snapped back to the present. Wade was already starting CPR.

Turning without a word, she dashed up the steps to the house.

"HE'LL LIVE," Wade said a few hours later as he sat down beside her on the cottage steps. She'd been deep in thought before he arrived. Her life had drastically changed in the blink of an eye, and she hardly knew how or where to start processing.

"That's good to know, I guess." She felt numb to the news.

"He'll likely spend the rest of his life in prison, if that's any consolation."

"A small one." She hugged her knees to her chest. "What about Lydia?"

"She claims she didn't know anything, though she must have suspected. Why else would she have left those notes if not to scare you away?"

"She admitted to writing the notes?" Abby shook her head in disbelief. "Of all the people in my life, I would never have guessed in a million years that my evil stepsister would be the one to try and save me."

"People are complicated," Wade said. "At least you now know what happened to your mother."

She nodded. "I need to go see my grandmother. I have to be the one to tell her about James."

"When will you leave?"

"In the morning." Abby sighed. "She'll want to plan a service. I can't even bear to think about that right now, but if it helps her get through this, then I'll go along with whatever she wants." She turned reluctantly from the water. "Can I ask you something?"

"Anything."

"Do you think your dad meant to leave town with my mother?"

Wade answered slowly. "I think he considered it but changed his mind at the last minute, just like James said."

"The affair is bound to come out at the trial," Abby said. "Have you thought about that?"

He nodded. "I won't be able to protect my mother from the truth. I think deep down she knows. She's probably always known."

Abby said softly, "So what comes next?"

He turned at that. "You tell me. You're leaving for Atlanta tomorrow. Is this goodbye?"

She couldn't bear the thought of never seeing him again. "I'll be coming back here in a few days. There are so many things to settle. The business, the properties. It'll take months to sort everything out. But what about you? Your business is done here."

"Not all of it. I think I'll stick around for a while, too."

"For your mom?"

"For a lot of reasons." He turned from the water to gaze down at her. "Not the least of which is this view."

Her heart started to thud. "Wade—"

"It's our time, Abby."

She sighed. "I've waited a long time to hear you say that."

"I've waited a long time to say it."

They exchanged a smile, and then he took her hand and entwined their fingers as they turned in unison to watch the sunset.

* * * * *